"Are you okay?" Cash murmured

Marley winced. "Not really. Uh…I guess it's because we're about to have sex."

He studied her a minute. "We don't have to."

She stared back, making him smile by saying, "Uh, yes, we do." And it was true. Neither of them would sleep until they'd satisfied their curiosity. "I'm just nervous."

"Me, too."

Maybe. But Marley didn't think Cash *looked* all that nervous. "It must be performance anxiety," she said, trying to make light of it.

His dark eyes sparkled as he pulled her close. "Yours or mine?"

Her jaw dropped. "Yours, of course."

He grinned. "Let me get this straight. You're afraid you're going to regret the best sex of your life…."

The tension in the room suddenly seemed palpable. Marley wanted to fast forward through all the groping and divesting of clothes. Truly, there was nothing worse than first-time sex, she thought.

But what if it did turn out to be the best sex…?

Dear Reader,

Since the early nineties I've been very lucky to have
been able to write for so many Harlequin series, including
Love & Laughter, American Romance, Intrigue, Blaze
and Temptation, as well as to pen what's been called the
BIG APPLE series, which has included miniseries such as
BIG APPLE BACHELORS and BIG APPLE BABIES.

These books are close to my heart, especially since I make
my home in Manhattan, and I have made my writing home,
for some time, at Harlequin Blaze and Harlequin Temptation,
which now brings you BIG APPLE BRIDES.

I do hope you'll enjoy watching the three Benning sisters
grapple with a wedding curse that's wreaked havoc with their
love lives. It's my greatest wish that they provide everything
for which the much-loved Temptation series has always
been known: sassiness, humorous fun, a fast pace and
a heartwarming happily-ever-after.

Enjoy!

Jule McBride

P.S. Next month look for *Nights in White Satin,* Bridget's story!

Books by Jule McBride

HARLEQUIN TEMPTATION
866—NAUGHTY BY NATURE
875—THE HOTSHOT*
883—THE SEDUCER*
891—THE PROTECTOR*
978—BEDSPELL

HARLEQUIN BLAZE
67—THE SEX FILES
91—ALL TUCKED IN

*The Big Apple Bachelors

JULE McBRIDE

SOMETHING BORROWED

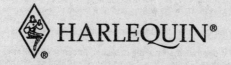

HARLEQUIN®

TORONTO • NEW YORK • LONDON
AMSTERDAM • PARIS • SYDNEY • HAMBURG
STOCKHOLM • ATHENS • TOKYO • MILAN • MADRID
PRAGUE • WARSAW • BUDAPEST • AUCKLAND

To Shlomo Nudel,
for being a voice of reason in the wilderness

ISBN 0-373-69205-6

SOMETHING BORROWED

Prologue

SPARKY DARDEN'S DAUGHTER, Julia, had fluffed his pillows, propping them against the headboard, just the way Sparky liked them, and she'd left a silver-wrapped square of chocolate on the coverlet like those left nightly on pillows of Darden hotels all over the world. As Sparky unwrapped the candy and popped it into his mouth, he reclined.

At the moment, he felt forty years old, not sixty-eight, and his cancer, which had gone into remission, wasn't worrying him in the least. As he ran his fingers through the remaining strands of silver hair left after chemo, he used his other hand to fish into the pocket of a crimson robe for the remote; he was tired of watching late-night infomercials, a habit acquired during his illness, so he switched to the VCR and hit Play.

Since the threats against Julia began, Sparky had watched this tape many times. Taken fourteen years ago by a security camera at the Long Island estate Sparky now called home, it was grainy and dark, so the figure racing across Sparky's lawn looked scarcely visible. The guy had been clever, breaching security, blackening his face and dressing in dark clothes. After locating the switch plates inside the estate's gates, he'd extinguished almost all the lights.

Cameras and alarms were everywhere, and with the exception of a wooded area between the house and a two-lane rural highway, fencing surrounded the property, but he'd been determined, climbing the fence, hurdling flower beds, dodging hedges and circling statuary. After reaching the veranda steps, he'd climbed stealthily, his body moving like a dancer's.

Inside, everyone had been shouting in confusion, trying to turn on the lights. Funny, Sparky thought now. He should have suspected foul play, since he'd made countless enemies in the course of his career, but he'd thought there was a power outage. "Nothing's wrong," he'd assured.

When he'd opened the door, though, a flashlight's beam from inside had glanced off steel. Just as air had whooshed across his exposed neck, he'd jumped back, realizing the wind had been the wake of a knife meant to slit his throat. And then he'd seen the eyes through the ski mask—dark and full of hate, as if the man had been fantasizing about this confrontation for years.

Sparky had lived, of course. Since starting Darden Enterprises, he'd survived murder attempts, near bankruptcy, paternity suits and slander, not to mention his own loneliness. The latter was like a gaping mouth inside him, and no matter what Sparky had fed it over the years—wine, women or song—he'd never felt filled. Always on to life's next conquest, he'd needed more sex, more money, more accolades. At least until he'd gotten the big C, and he'd survived that, too.

After rewinding the video, he watched once more as the shadowy figure reached to his waist, unsnapped a sheath and pulled out the knife. After that, the black-clad man leaned, lifted the door knocker and let it fall.

Had fourteen years really passed since that night? They seemed lost in a blur of champagne fountains, caviar and high-heeled women who'd been half Sparky's age. In his mind's eye, he always saw himself stepping from private planes, buying expensive suits, or cutting ribbons at hotels, new ventures that always signified a business deal where someone else got screwed in the end. He'd made so many enemies. The man who'd come to kill him that night was only one.

Sparky's daughter by the only woman he'd married was the bright light in it all. He'd lay down his life for her and his enemies knew it. Did the man in the video still hold a grudge? Finally, after all these years, a private eye had gotten close to discovering who he was, but would they actually locate him before Julia's upcoming wedding? And should Sparky tell Julia's bodyguard, Pete Shriver, about this old video, or wait until the P.I. found the man? This piece of dirty laundry wasn't one Sparky wanted to air, after all. The man's vendetta had been too personal....

Which was why Sparky had let him go. Now he damned himself for showing uncharacteristic mercy. Why hadn't he treated his near-killer to the same ruthlessness he employed in business?

And was the past really coming back to haunt him? Was the man about to call again, drawn by Julia's highly publicized wedding? Wishing he hadn't pushed to give his daughter the wedding of the year, Sparky dragged his fingers thoughtfully over his scalp. Julia was so in love with her fiancé, Lorenzo Santini, that she'd have happily eloped. Maybe Sparky should have let her.

"Julia," he whispered on a sigh. By insisting on such a large wedding had he made his daughter a target?

1

STOP THE WEDDING or the bride will die.

Lifting her gaze from the letter on the boardroom table, wedding planner Edie Benning glanced at Emma Goldstein, a writer from *Celebrity Wedding* magazine, then toward Julia Darden, but the bride-to-be only continued kissing her fiancé. Julia and Lorenzo weren't the brightest couple, but their passion could melt Siberia. Still, Edie was surprised when they didn't stop kissing to voice concern for their safety. Not that Edie would mention it, since Julia's daddy, Sparky, CEO of the Darden hotel empire, had given Edie carte blanche to create New York's best-ever wedding, an event that could make her a real player in Manhattan wedding-planning circles.

The responsibility would have been daunting under any circumstances, but as Julia's bodyguard, Pete Shriver, slid another letter across the table, Edie felt her dream of building a business slipping through her fingers.

"Someone wants to put a damper on the wedding," Pete announced, "so we're going to tighten security around Julia."

Edie just hoped Pete wouldn't suggest the couple

nix the celebration and elope for safety reasons. The couple was still making out, and since Edie's love life sucked, the smoochy-face was hard to take. During the month since she'd started dating a guy from New Orleans named Cash Champagne, Cash hadn't even tried to progress things beyond their few lackluster kisses. It was the sort of thing that made Edie feel sure her Granny Ginny wasn't telling tall tales; clearly, just as her sisters Marley and Bridget had always believed, and as Granny had proclaimed, the Bennings really were victims of a wedding curse.

"From now on, Edie," Pete was saying, "Marley needs to give Julia her morning workouts at the Darden estate. Julia and Lorenzo were already in the city, so they could meet us tonight, but until we catch whoever's sending the letters, Julia should stay in Long Island. We found out the guy's mailing the letters from a box on East Ninety-Sixth Street, so hopefully, we'll catch him soon...."

"I'm sure Marley won't mind coming to the estate." At least Edie hoped not. But who knew? Edie had done everything to help her twin get back on her feet after her divorce, including giving Marley this opportunity to be Julia Darden's personal trainer, but Marley, who'd become hopelessly cynical since her divorce, hadn't even said thank you.

The rest of the family made up for it. Edie's father, Joe, was catering the affair, and her mother, Viv, a seamstress, was making gowns; Edie's youngest sister, Bridget, worked at Tiffany's and was producing ring designs. Despite the excitement, Marley kept saying Edie's luck in landing this assignment was too good to be true. No man as wealthy as Sparky Darden would take a chance on an unknown such as Edie, Marley had argued.

Ever since her divorce, she'd been difficult, especially when it came to accepting help from Edie. She also distrusted anyone Edie dated, something Edie understood since Marley's ex had wiped out the funds from Marley's fitness club, Fancy Abs, putting Marley out of business. As far as Edie was concerned, the end of the marriage had been brutal, even by the high standards set by other Benning-sister breakups. Yes, when it came to marriage, the Bennings were definitely cursed….

Edie cast a glance at Emma Goldstein, who was taking notes, and continued, "At Big Apple Brides, we'll do everything to ensure Julia's safety."

"It's appreciated," Pete returned. "The letters have been coming since October when the wedding was announced."

Edie frowned. "You weren't worried then?"

"We stepped up security, but with the wedding so close…"

Six months wasn't enough time to plan, but Julia would only agree to the April date, now three months away. As near as Edie could tell, the heiress would elope tomorrow, but she hadn't done so because she wanted to please her father.

"Go ahead with your plans, Edie," encouraged Pete. "My guess is Julia's not the real target. Probably, the letters are from an old business rival of Mr. Darden's, someone hoping to cast a cloud over the big day, but who doesn't want to hurt Julia. Most perpetrators with serious intent don't pussyfoot around like this. And Sparky will be the first to admit he's made enemies. We need to take more precautions, though."

"I didn't mention it, but…"

Pete's eyes narrowed. "What?"

Edie shook her head, thinking she was being paranoid. "Maybe I'm just nervous, but in the past few days, I've felt…as if someone might be outside the shop watching me…."

"Hudson Street stays busy."

Edie cast a glance toward the conference room's open door, the windows and crowded street. Despite the circumstances, she couldn't help but congratulate herself. Her business was impressive. No one would guess the Bennings had redone the interior of Big Apple Brides themselves, the women painting while Joe carpeted the floors and built shelves that were now lined with wedding books.

The windows were her mother's idea. On one, the words *Big Apple Brides* were painted in gold. Draped with satin swags, both glassed cases brimmed with wedding items: champagne glasses, a hope chest, garters and bouquets. A winged mannequin wore a gown of white feathers, a bed waited in invitation, and roses were strewn across the floor. The effect was pure fantasy, inviting couples to create their ultimate dreams. Not that the ambiance had done anything for Edie's love life, of course. How could it, she thought with a sudden rush of pique, when a century-old curse ensured failure in the area of romance?

Pushing aside the thought, she stared at the corner of Hudson and Perry Streets. "The street's especially busy now," she continued. It was late January, but after-Christmas shoppers were still combing stores for sales.

"I'll have a man check in with you once a day. Okay?"

Nodding, Edie glanced toward the bride, who was shooting Lorenzo a dazzling smile. Julia was beautiful. Taller than average and model-slender, she had brown eyes, a clear complexion and an unusually wide mouth. Despite being camera shy, her looks had made her a media darling. Lorenzo was no slouch, either. The pro hockey player could have body-doubled for Benicio Del Toro.

Months ago, the lives of the rich and famous had been the furthest thing from Edie's mind; her main focus had been opening the wedding boutique and involving her family members. All the Bennings knew this was Edie's way of counteracting the curse. Years ago, Edie had thought Granny Ginny was only being entertaining, of course, but as time wore on, Edie had never fallen in love, Marley had divorced, and their youngest sister, Bridget, had actually applied to the *Guinness Book of World Records,* hoping to be recognized for having survived the most bad dates in Manhattan.

Edie was sure that sending good wedding karma into the Universe by planning weddings would turn the tide for the Benning sisters, and so far, things seemed positive. Even if the chemistry wasn't right, at least she'd gotten some dates with a real hunk, right? And while her relatives weren't technically employees, they'd begun to offer their skills, which meant Edie now had talented, trustworthy subcontractors at her fingertips.

"At least you got a restraining order for Jimmy Delaney," Emma was saying, addressing the next order of business.

Since the wedding announcement, Julia had become a magnet for paparazzi, and Jimmy Delaney was the most persistent photographer. Pete looked proud of himself. "Yeah."

"Only photographers from *Celebrity Weddings* can cover the event," reminded Emma. "We have the exclusive."

"Delaney won't get near the estate," Pete assured.

"Lighten up!" Julia interjected with a laugh, breaking a kiss and pulling her gaze from Lorenzo with difficulty. "I thought this was supposed to be a wedding!"

Lorenzo leaned over, tugging the bill of a baseball cap Julia wore with old jeans and a sports-logo sweatshirt. She'd draped a Gore-Tex jacket around the back of her chair. His eyes never leaving hers, Lorenzo said, "Let's start talking hearts and flowers. If I don't marry this lady soon, I really will die." Crossing a finger over his heart, he shot everyone a lovesick expression.

Edie smiled. "You're in luck, Lorenzo. I brought more tapes for review. And about the ring." She slid drawings toward the couple. "We're hoping you'll approve...."

"You need to decide," urged Emma. "Our next article appears soon, and while readers have loved sharing the pressures of a rushed celebrity wedding, they want to see results."

"The wedding's going to be amazing," assured Julia.

Not if she didn't choose the music, thought Edie uneasily. And the ring. On so many other points, Julia had been amiable. The cake she'd approved was a design Edie had initially conjured for her own fantasy wedding. The traditional gown was perfect, and the pink roses twined with lavender glass beads. Edie just wished the wedding wasn't in April. The wedding and reception were at the estate, and Edie didn't know what to expect—a blizzard or spring rain.

Julia gasped. "Look, Lozo." Lozo was her pet name for Lorenzo.

Unbidden, Edie's heart pulled. These two were so in love that they'd marry happily with no ceremony, much less a ring. Lorenzo had proposed with a pop-can lid, now silver-plated and hanging from a chain around Julia's neck. It would be on Julia's finger if Sparky hadn't insisted that his daughter have a diamond.

Edie still couldn't understand why Julia had rejected the first designs. While Big Apple Brides really wasn't officially a family business, Edie's relatives were helping with the Darden wedding, a trend Edie hoped would continue since she was picking up clients daily, and she really appreciated how Bridget had gone the distance.

Working around her hours as a clerk at Tiffany's, Bridget, the youngest sister, had put her heart and soul into the ring design, and the initial offering had wowed even Marley, which was saying something. Sure that Julia would be impressed, Bridget had commissioned a model made of cubic zirconia, but Julia had rejected it, after all, and now Bridget was wearing the ring, which was sort of pathetic, Edie decided. Just as determined as Edie to counteract the wedding curse, it was as if Bridget had placed an engagement ring on her own finger....

"This is it," Julia announced.

The ring wasn't as beautiful as Bridget's first design in Edie's opinion, but it was impressive, as was Lorenzo's band. "The diamonds will be of the best quality," Edie assured. "Set at Tiffany's."

Julia flashed a grin. "Great!"

"Oh," cut in Emma. "Before I forget. Since you're going on *Rate the Dates* after this meeting, Edie, I want *Celebrity Wedding*'s photographers to meet you at the studio. Okay?"

Edie wondered what to say. Just days after she'd been hired by the Dardens, *Celebrity Weddings* had phoned, asking for exclusive rights to cover the wedding. In turn, Edie had broached the subject with the Dardens, feeling sure they'd decline, only to find that Sparky was ecstatic. Despite Julia's camera-shyness, he wanted her to have the documentation of her special day forever. Well and good. But one thing had led to another, and *Celebrity Weddings*—which had been a bit pushy—wanted Edie and Cash, a man she'd only casually dated, to appear on a nationally televised reality show called *Rate the Dates*.

"Just audition, Edie," Emma had urged at the time. "It's a promotional thing and you can always cancel. Since it's a weekly show and airs live, they have alternates waiting in the wings."

On the show, newly acquainted couples were videotaped during dream dates in Manhattan while a studio audience and two-person judging panel rated their likelihood of sharing a future. So the audience could see how well it had judged, each show included a segment called "Where Are They Today?" By generating interest in Edie's love life, *Celebrity Weddings* hoped to boost circulation for the issues covering Julia and Lorenzo, and when the idea was initially broached, Edie decided to do it, since she might get new clients.

But then she'd come to her senses. After all, the Benning sisters were affected by a wedding curse, something proven by their lifelong histories of bad dates, which meant Edie's appearance on *Rate the Dates* could backfire. If Julia's wedding was somehow tainted, Edie would never forgive herself.

Feeling a rush of guilt, Edie told herself she was being ridiculous. Surely curses couldn't rub off on third parties. Still, from a practical standpoint, it was better not to complicate matters by focusing on her own romantic life while planning this wedding. She didn't need any distractions, which was another good reason to quit dating Cash Champagne.

Yes…she'd concentrate on only one wedding— Julia's. When it came off perfectly, that would prove to Granny Ginny and Edie's sisters that the Benning name was to be associated with marital bliss—not tales of spinsterhood.

"Emma," Edie said with conviction. "I've thought about it, and I'm going to cancel. As you say, *Rate the Dates* always has alternates." Deciding not to mention the unpromising, dry-as-dust kisses she'd shared with Cash, Edie added, "Cash and I only dated a month."

"That's the point," argued Emma. "Contestants *get* to know their dates while America watches!"

Edie hardly wanted America to witness her and Cash's lack of passion on TV. Besides, as far as her sisters went, any failure would be interpreted as proof that they were cursed and never likely to marry. "No, I *really* can't appear." Refusing to consider the show's hefty grand prize, a sum that would help with the overhead at Big Apple Brides, Edie continued, "Marley's going to let Cash know."

She wished she'd been able to track him down herself, but the man was definitely elusive. And the way the day had progressed, ending in this impromptu meeting, finding him had been impossible. Frowning at her watch, she wondered if Marley had succeeded yet, and then why her twin had been so unusually helpful. Since her divorce, Marley had viewed men suspiciously, but today, she'd seemed almost eager to help Edie find Cash. Well, maybe it was because Edie had decided not to appear with him on *Rate the Dates*, despite the sizable grand prize….

As she approached Rockefeller Center and NBC, Marley tried to ignore the fact that the hike uptown had made her thirsty, and she wished she had time to stop for water, but she didn't. Catching a glimpse in Saks' window, she barely recognized herself. Was she really wearing press-on nails, sheer pantyhose that couldn't protect her legs from the biting wind, and black pointy-toed come-love-me heels that were cutting off circulation from her toes to her hips and probably damaging her sciatic nerve?

Her usually curly hair was blown out straight— her arms ached from an hour's work with the hair dryer—and because she was wearing a fur coat, her twin's pride and joy, she'd already been accosted by an animal rights activist who'd followed her from West Fourth to Thirty-Fourth Street station, educating Marley about the trials and tribulations of being a mink.

Marley had finally lost her temper and explained that she was only human, which meant she didn't feel competent to speak for minks. However, she could definitely say it wasn't easy being *her*. She'd proceeded to tell the activist about the wedding curse that had ruined her marriage, offering details about her divorce before bringing the man up to the present, explaining that she was impersonating someone else right now, so this wasn't even her coat. Besides, the coat wasn't mink, she'd informed him, but beaver, and it had been bought by her sister second-hand, so her sister wasn't responsible for an animal death, at least not directly.

The coat was hanging over an itchy red-wool suit that reminded Marley of why she favored clothes made of cotton. As it turned out, that was something she and the man had in common, and on that basis, he'd asked for a date, but Marley had declined, quickly reminding him of the wedding curse. As much as she missed sex and romance, the curse was a reality—her divorce proved that—so she really did feel compelled to swear off men forever.

Now she just hoped she could help Edie. She definitely looked like her now; before she'd left the West Village where her parents and Edie lived, she'd passed the deli, the drop-off laundry and a restaurant where the Bennings often ordered takeout, and no one had seen through the disguise.

Still, she was second-guessing her plan to show up at NBC and fool Edie's latest boyfriend into thinking she was Edie. "But you don't have a choice," Marley reminded herself, licking at lips that felt like cotton. She had to stop her sister from making a devastating mistake, such as the one Marley had made when she'd married Chris Lang. Edie was too much of a romantic to see through Cash Champagne's surface charm....

And Cash definitely had some ulterior motive in dating Edie. Not only did Cash Champagne sound like a stage name worthy of a Broadway show, but he didn't seem to have reliable employment, either, just like Marley's ex-husband, Chris. And his looks were too good to be true, at least judging from the few times Marley had seen him. He did, however, seem to be from New Orleans—his accent indicated that was the truth—but the way he'd appeared in the Bennings' lives was fishy, so Marley just wanted the chance to probe deeper into his background than Edie seemed willing to do....

Marley lowered her head as she crossed Fifth Avenue, holding her stiff hair-sprayed locks in place with both hands and keeping her eyes glued to the pavement, hoping one of Edie's high heels wouldn't catch in a subway grate and send her sprawling. No, poor Edie just didn't get it. She was still such a romantic fool.

While Marley didn't want to be condescending, she couldn't help but feel her twin—who was older by two minutes—was really years younger. Despite the wedding curse that Granny Ginny had said ensured their failure in romance, everything remained hearts, flowers and happy endings for Edie. She still fantasized about the perfect wedding day—the sun shining, spring flowers blooming, a tall, dark, handsome man who looked like Cash Champagne waiting at the end of the aisle....

Oh, Marley and Edie might not hang around together as much as they used to, and they'd always had different friends, but Marley would hate to see her twin get hurt. She felt a pang in her chest as she visualized Big Apple Brides' display windows and thought of the loving care that Edie, not to mention all the Bennings, had put into the business, despite the fact that none of the sisters were destined for success in love.

Only Marley had made the mistake of marrying. Refusing to give credence to old family stories, she'd seen her love for Chris Lang as proof the curse didn't exist. Only a year ago, while signing divorce papers, had she smelled the coffee. Obviously, Granny hadn't been spinning wild yarns as the sisters had sometimes hoped, and until this curse was resolved, Marley, Edie and Bridget were destined to be alone. For that reason, Marley was glad her elderly relative was coming in from Florida this week. Now that she took the curse more seriously, maybe Marley and her sisters could ask Granny Ginny how to rectify matters.

As things stood, Cash Champagne was just one more heartbreaker who'd wind up harming Edie. Not that Marley cared about her own love life any longer. What was the use? In fact, she wanted as little to do with weddings as possible, which was why she wished she had any other option besides working as Julia Darden's fitness trainer.

Fortunately, Marley had almost rebuilt the clientele she'd had when Chris depleted their joint bank account, and she'd had to close her spa center, Fancy Abs. As difficult as it was to listen to Julia's deluded chatter about gowns and crystal, Marley always refrained from reciting divorce statistics since she desperately needed the job. She was working in clients' apartments right now, and unless she could open a commercial space soon, people would switch to the new fitness franchises springing up all over Manhattan.

Bitter air hit the back of her throat, making her even thirstier as she wrapped Edie's coat more tightly around herself and headed past the Sea Grill restaurant. Silently, she damned her throat for feeling so achy. She really didn't have time to stop for something to drink, and if the truth be told, a martini was starting to sound better than a bottle of Evian. She heaved a sigh. Why did Edie always wear short skirts? And such sheer hose? Her sister was so impractical!

A month ago, when six feet of pure temptation had waltzed into Edie's life calling himself Cash Champagne, Edie had taken that as a positive sign. At least at first. Admittedly, he was a dream to look at, his body big and hard with muscles, his dark eyes always squinting as if he were staring into sunlight, his lips curling into absent smiles as if to say he'd seen it all and nothing surprised him. Not exactly the kind of man who dated women slated to be old maids.

But what was wrong with being single, anyway? Marley suddenly fumed. Throughout history, countless women traversed the years when, as Florence Nightingale had put it, "forever turned into never." The Bennings were hardly the first. Many "bachelor girls" wound up happier, able to concentrate on their own life goals. Which was what Marley intended to do....

When she, Edie and Bridget had met Cash last

month in an East Village comedy club, Marley had reacted on a purely physical level, of course. In fact, when he'd sent a round of drinks, then headed toward their group, she'd been sure her smile had lured him. Just as she was kicking herself for flirting accidently, the low, sexy rumble of his voice had helped bring her to her senses, reminding her of her divorce, and everything that she'd gone through in the past year.

Luckily, the following morning, she'd scheduled a workout with a TV executive who could refer more clients, so she'd been unable to stay at the club and seduce Cash. She did remain long enough to realize he'd never even heard of the feminist stand-up act—a local talent. He'd seemed out of place, too, a lone man surrounded by a female audience enjoying jokes about hair loss, penis size and men's bizarre relationships with their electronic equipment.

Because the dingy pub—an old speakeasy sandwiched between buildings on Avenue A—would have been impossible for a tourist to find, Marley couldn't figure out how Cash had come to be there, especially since he'd had no interest in comedy or the performer, and he knew no one. He wasn't drinking alcohol, either, only club soda, which seemed odd, since he'd said he'd gotten his start as a bartender, then worked his way up to owning his own clubs, and Marley had never met a teetotaling bartender.

He'd chuckled at appropriate places, but his eyes had remained veiled, maybe even calculating, and Marley had gotten the impression he was deciding which sister he'd like to know, rather than letting events take their natural course. For some reason, she'd found herself imagining a scenario in which he'd followed them to the club, intending to pick up one of them....

Surely, she was wrong. And yet she'd wound up concluding that something was up his sleeve. Edie would say that was only because Marley's breakup with Chris had scarred her emotionally. Now she thought back, trying to remember if she'd seen Cash before their meeting in the pub. Had he been in a deli? A café? No matter how often she'd replayed that night, picturing herself and her sisters meeting at their parents' apartment, walking to Seventh Avenue and catching a cab to the East Side, she couldn't remember seeing him on the street....

Cash had quickly passed on Marley as a prospect, though. She did remember that clearly. When she'd said she was leaving, he'd turned his attention to Bridget, who was the most obvious of the sisters, the one men always looked at first. Her outfits were flashier and her voice louder, probably because she'd felt left out when they were kids, overshadowed by twin sisters who had—at least back then—been inseparable. But Bridget had been talking to a friend on her cell, which meant Cash's attention had shifted once more, this time to Edie, who was clearly wowed by his looks.

That was when Marley had left. Now, all she knew was what she'd gleaned from her tight-lipped sister who hadn't divulged much except that Cash was a lousy kisser. Given his devil's grin, dripping dark locks and swaggering walk, Marley had figured him for a ladies' man, the kind of guy who'd know how to make a woman feel like a woman.

"TMI!" Marley had protested when Edie had divulged the gossip about the kisses. "Too much information!"

"I know I should quit seeing him. There's just no chemistry. But he's so good-looking that I keep hoping…" Edie had paused. "Is being a bad kisser really a fatal flaw?"

"Yes!" exclaimed both Bridget and Marley in unison, and then Bridget had added, "but guys who look like that always get plenty of practice, so I just don't get it."

Marley had hesitated, unwilling to state the obvious, since it might spoil their good moods, but she had felt compelled to say, "The wedding curse. That must be it. Maybe he's a great kisser, just not when he kisses one of us. Uh, you know, a Benning."

Edie had groaned. "Don't start with that again."

"Marley does have a point," Bridget had said, her blue eyes growing distant as if she were staring at a far-off partner whom she'd never really meet, face-to-face.

Now Marley winced at Edie's watch as she pushed through a revolving door at NBC. Fifteen minutes until six, she thought. It was later than she'd imagined, almost the time Edie had been told to arrive at the studio. At least the timing ensured Cash would be here already.

But where? In the lobby, a line of people was preparing to be led upstairs, and judging from the signs they carried, they were the studio audience for *Rate the Dates.* Slipping past them, Marley headed for an open elevator, following directions Edie had given. When she reached an attendant wearing green slacks and a matching blazer, she announced herself, saying, "Edie Benning," and then she watched in relief as the woman crossed her off a guest list.

"I'll phone upstairs and tell them you're finally here," the woman said.

Finally? Marley thought a moment later as the elevator car ascended. The woman had made it sound as if Marley were late, but hadn't Edie said to be here by six, since the show started at seven? Suddenly, Marley wished she'd asked for more information. Had Cash possibly changed his mind, anyway? After all, Edie had said alternates were always ready to go on, which meant last-minute cancellation wasn't supposed to be a problem. Besides, Cash had been reticent about going on the air, anyway.

But what if he tried to strong-arm her into appearing for some reason? In that case, should she tell him she wasn't Edie? Marley felt a sudden stab of panic. Should she have come earlier? Had Edie gotten her facts wrong? Swallowing with difficulty, since her mouth was still bone dry, Marley felt a rush of pique at Cash Champagne. As far as she was concerned, all this aggravation was his fault. If he'd answered his cell phone, Edie could have canceled herself. Men were all alike, Marley thought. So many never grew up, living long into adulthood at the center of their own little worlds....

Edie had been trying to call Cash all day, but he'd hardly cared that his unavailability might affect *her,* much less Marley who was now tracking him down. As soon as she'd spoken with Edie, Marley had meant to head straight to Cash's supposed work site—a new Upper West Side club called the Plantation House, a fancy restaurant-bar he'd said he was opening with an old friend—but then she'd decided to disguise herself as Edie. She just wanted the opportunity to size him up at length, to make sure Edie wasn't making a mistake by dating him.

Dressing had taken longer than anticipated. She and Edie had been born identical, but they'd evolved different tastes and lifestyles that, today, made them look more like sisters than twins. Because Marley had a slightly heavier, more muscular body from working out, not all Edie's clothes fit, and even after she'd dressed, shoes remained a problem since Edie's closet was organized with boxes bearing coded labels only she could understand. As far as Marley was concerned, you'd need a cryptanalyst from the CIA to decipher Edie's closet. Just as Marley had found shoes, she'd realized she needed to clip her bangs if she was going to look like Edie....

In the end, the disguise was perfect. Unfortunately, that meant Edie's neighbors had stopped Marley, wanting to chat. By the time she reached the subway, the animal rights activist had accosted her, and when she got out at Times Square, the afternoon's beautiful dusting of snow had turned to sleet in the twilight, and she hadn't been able to get a cab the rest of the way to Fiftieth.

"Just tell Cash I can't be on the show," Edie had said, making it sound so easy. "He won't mind," she'd assured. "To tell you the truth, I had to talk him into it. I was excited about it at the time. He didn't even seem interested in the prize money."

"Aren't you?" Marley had asked, thinking about how she, herself, could use the money to start her fitness center.

Edie had hesitated. "Yeah," she'd finally admitted. "But I don't think I should go on the show. I mean, like I said, Cash and I don't really seem to be clicking...."

Marley could see why Edie kept hanging on. The guy was gorgeous. But why was Cash still interested if there wasn't any chemistry? When the elevator doors opened onto a hallway packed with people, there was no more time to ponder the question. Another woman in a green blazer and slacks, positioned at the elevator, said, "You are?"

"Mar—uh, Edie Benning."

Just as she glanced around, looking for Cash, she felt a surprisingly strong hand close around her upper arm and when she glanced up, she was staring into the face of a tall man with short dark hair named Trevor Milane, whom she recognized as the host for the reality show. Not that Marley had actually seen a full episode of *Rate the Dates*, only ads for it, many of which were on public buses. Before she could introduce herself, the man, who looked astonishingly like Pierce Brosnan said, "Where have you been? Don't you know our show is nationally televised? Oh, it doesn't matter, just get back to costume."

The hallway was so crowded, Marley could barely move, much less find a costume department. "I came to cancel," she managed to say. "I need to find Cash Champagne."

"Cancel?" Trevor growled, thrusting harried fingers through his dark hair as he spun abruptly and half dragged her down the hallway, wending around studio workers, his grip firm even when she tried to shake it off. "Keep dreaming, sweetheart," he said gruffly, still pulling her along. "We air live, and there's no time left." He raised his voice. "Contestant six finally made it," he called, his gravelly voice now turning magically soft in a heartbeat, the deep baritone almost as sexy as Cash Champagne's. It was as if he'd said, "Open sesame."

Double doors opened on the studio, and Marley's jaw slackened as she stared into the insanity beyond. People were ducking and circling each other, carrying everything from legal pads to technical equipment; the same line of people she'd seen in the lobby were now being marshaled into studio seats by more women in green slacks and blazers.

Nearer, someone gasped and said, "Thank God she's dressed."

Someone else groaned. "Red will blend with the backdrop."

Just as Marley realized they were talking about her suit, another disembodied voice hit her ears, saying, "Less than six minutes until airtime!" Her mouth still feeling like cotton, she started to ask for water, but her attention was diverted by still another voice, adding, "Trevor says to change the swivel chairs on stage to blue, not red. Otherwise, she'll blend."

Blend? God forbid. Reaching, Marley grabbed the first arm she could, the crowded space near the doors so thick with people that she wasn't sure if the eyes into which she stared imploringly were really connected to the arm she held. "Look," she managed to say. "It's sounds as if you're close to airtime, but I need to cancel. Uh...you said you had alternates. I was told to be here at six—"

"Exactly. Why weren't you?"

She stared at Edie's watch. "I was. I am. I mean—"

"Five until airtime!" said the voice.

"It's seven o'clock, Ms. Benning. You're an hour late," someone else said.

Marley was pulling the watch to her ear. Sure enough, it had stopped. Her heart thudded in panic. She couldn't appear on *Rate the Dates*, no way. "I need to find my…uh…date. His name's Cash Champagne. There's been a mistake."

"Four minutes!"

How could time be flying so fast? Surely a minute hadn't passed! As Marley drew a sharp breath, Edie's coat was whisked from her shoulders. "Please," she managed to say, fighting rising panic. "I need that coat." Edie would kill her if she lost it.

No response came, but a bottled water was thrust into her hand. That she could use. Gulping, she felt the cool water slide down her throat as a sheet on a clipboard was put in front of her, and someone said, "Here, Edie. If you'll just sign…"

Even though she thought it was rude to make contestants sign for drinks, especially water, she scribbled her sister's name, took a deep breath, and said, "Thanks. I was thirsty."

"Take these, too," someone said, handing her a health bar just as a hand came over her shoulder.

"Two-sided tape," another voice said behind her. "I'm attaching it to your blouse. It'll hold the microphone."

"Microphone?"

"At least she blow-dried her own hair," someone said.

"According to the initial interview, she has natural curls."

"That skirt's too short, though. She can't go on in that."

"I'm not going on," Marley said, beginning to realize that it was pointless to protest.

"Three minutes," someone shouted.

"Your skirt's really short, so make sure your knees are pressed together, Ms. Benning."

The idea of exposing her panties to America sent another wave of panic through her system. Marley craned her neck toward the elevators, wondering if she should run. "Where's Cash? I've got to talk to him."

"All couples want to talk before the show," another woman soothed. "But in just a minute, you'll see him onstage—"

"No! I just came to—"

A woman moved quickly in front of her, unwrapped the health bar, tore off a piece and pushed it into Marley's mouth, leaving Marley only one option—to chew and swallow, at least if she wanted to talk again. "Atta, girl," said the woman. "For most contestants, eating right before you go on the air helps. Now smile. Let me check your teeth."

This was becoming more surreal by the moment. "Please," Marley managed to say. "I'm not going to be on your show. Now, if you don't mind, I really have to talk to someone in charge."

The only response was a comb. Someone behind her dragged it through her hair, then re-shellacked the locks with another wave of thick hair spray. Even worse, she felt someone grasp her hand and start to apply nail polish to Edie's press-on nails, saying, "It won't dry this close to airtime, but you can just rest your hands on your thighs."

Was the woman out of her mind? Marley never painted her nails, so she was hardly practiced about how to let them dry while she was on TV. "What was wrong with them?" she asked.

"The color's wrong for your suit. And this will make them look less like press-ons."

"Please," Marley said. "Just don't put on the polish." She'd never worn red polish in her life.

"All the other women are polished."

But she wasn't going onstage with the other women! The show was televised for a week! If she went on tonight, she imagined she'd be locked into the other shows, also. And she wasn't even Edie. As Marley parted her lips to speak, an attendant started glossing them with something that smelled like strawberries. "You don't seem to understand!" Marley managed to say futilely, frustration lifting her voice an octave.

"Two minutes!"

The words echoed in her mind. She had to get out of here. Straining her eyes past whoever was fiddling with the collar of her silk blouse, she glimpsed Edie's watch again. How could this be? How could her efficient sister not have realized her watch had stopped? The hands hadn't budged. As Marley lifted the watch to her ear, her wrists were spritzed with a scent that reminded her of spring rain. She simply couldn't believe this. Marley's hyper-organized sister actually took her watches to the jeweler biannually, just for a battery checkups.

Truly, she felt like Alice after she'd stepped

through the looking glass. The hallway was still packed with people, too, and the scents of bodies, not to mention the cloying mix of perfumes and colognes, was making Marley's stomach start to churn. Sheer hysteria was making her feel woozy, and her chest had constricted as if a vise had tightened around her rib cage.

The voice came again. "One minute!"

"Get her into the green room!"

"Please," Marley said as someone pushed her from behind. "Just let me talk to Cash. I'm sure he doesn't really want to be on the show, either."

"Are you kidding?" the woman with the health bar soothed. "He's waiting in the blue room where we put the men. He keeps asking if you've arrived."

Marley considered fighting her way out, simply storming through the hallway, knocking aside whoever was in her path. She could, of course. She worked out all day. She was thoroughly hydrated, her muscles toned. She had stamina. But whatever she did would reflect badly on her sister, including announcing to the NBC staff that she wasn't really Edie. Her own business had already folded, so she'd hate to see her sister's meet the same fate.

Telling herself to stay calm, she took another deep breath as yet another door opened in front of her. Ah, she thought, the green room. Across the stage, she realized, was another large, boxlike room, which was blue; presumably the men were inside.

Here, the walls and floors were the color of Marley's Italian bicycle, a sea-foam-green color the bicycle company had named Celeste. Wishfully thinking she was on her bike and pedaling out of here, Marley stared at the two women inside—a grinning, curvy woman with wild dark hair, and a tall, thin, square-jawed blonde, who was tanned and wearing all white.

Marley startled when the door of the green room shut behind her; only one of the attendants remained. As she began straightening the collar of the blond woman's outfit, Marley wondered what to do next. She'd only seen snippets of this show, but she was familiar with the premise—contestants went on a week of dream dates while a studio audience judged whether the relationship would blossom into long-term romance. What had Edie been thinking? Would anyone—much less a woman affected by a wedding curse who was a proven failure at love—want her fledgling romance held up to scrutiny?

Oh, yes. She could definitely see why Edie wanted to cancel. Suddenly, relief flooded her. "You have alternates," she said to the attendant who'd remained in the green room.

The woman only shook her head. "They left as soon as you got here."

"Left?" Marley felt the floor being whisked from beneath her feet. For a moment, she couldn't even find her voice. "W-what if a contestant has a heart attack right after she gets here?" she sputtered.

"You're not having a heart attack, Edie," the woman said flatly.

Vaguely, Marley was aware that the show was airing now. From inside the box, she couldn't hear anything, but a small TV was affixed to the ceiling. Trevor Milane was addressing the studio audience. Her heart was racing, her mind whirling with confusion. She couldn't go on a reality show dressed like her twin—especially not when she'd come here to break a date for her.

"Thirty seconds!"

Marley watched in panic as, on the mounted television, the door of the green box was opened by an attendant. The studio audience went wild, offering whistles and hoots while clapping their hands and stomping their feet. Her heart felt as if it were dropping to her feet. One of the many voices she'd just heard replayed in her mind. *Just follow the lead of the other contestants.* Knowing she had no other choice, Marley somehow managed to put one foot in front of the other, scarcely believing any of this was really happening. Only the wedding curse could have made her plan to impersonate Edie backfire this drastically, and she could only hope their parents weren't watching....

"Welcome to *Rate the Dates*," Trevor Milane was saying as she and the other women filed past. He really was incredibly good-looking, and Marley could only hope she'd stop noticing such things sometime soon. A smile that didn't quit and a designer jacket had transformed the gruff man from the hallway into Mr. Charm, one of TV's prime-time reality-show celebrities. While she'd only seen snippets of the show, and ads for it, she knew Trevor was a regular. Each week, he hosted with a young woman chosen from contestants around the country. Now, he was grinning at a cute, corn-fed blonde beside him, saying, "And now that the women are seated, we're ready to bring in the lucky males."

As Marley seated herself, time ground to a halt,

and for a fleeting second, she felt it was the world, not Edie's watch, that had stopped. And then everything started moving again, every sound in the studio impossibly loud.

Everything looked overly bright, too, garish and surreal. Bright blinding lights were in her eyes, so she couldn't really see the audience, something she hadn't anticipated. When she saw herself on a large, wall-mounted screen behind the hosts, her heart thudded harder. She really did look like Edie! While Edie wore her blond hair blown out straight, Marley usually kept hers in a disarray of waves. And while Edie favored tailored suits with designer labels, Marley wore ancient, ripped sweatpants and torn T-shirts looking, Edie always said, like a throwback from the movie *Flashdance*. Even their own mother said Marley's outfits weren't fit for the trash. Due to their stylistic differences, strangers never thought Edie and Marley were sisters, much less identical twins. But now...

Marley bit back another rush of panic as the men came closer. Her head was swimming, her tummy tumbling with butterflies. None of this was supposed to be happening. Even worse, if she tried to explain this to Edie, saying she'd meant to interrogate Cash, since she feared Edie couldn't protect herself, Edie would be even angrier.

Her heart missed a beat. Her throat went dry again. And then the whole world slid sideways. For a second, she could swear she was about to faint. Instead, she managed to exhale another quick breath as Cash paused, almost missing a step, his gaze dropping seductively down the front of her dress, as if he were already playing for the cameras.

It was the wrong time to remember how his eyes had drifted over her in the comedy club. Or how he'd stared at her when she'd met him once more, inside Big Apple Brides, and yet another time when he'd offered her a ride in his truck, which she'd declined. Shaking her head, hoping to clear it of conclusion, she recalled how Edie had begged her to get new clothes for working out with Julia Darden, and Marley had. Lots of little tops and spandex pants, which was what she'd been wearing the last time she'd seen Cash....

Of course he wouldn't remember that, though. Because he thought she was Edie. He slid beside her, and she actually shuddered when his powerful arm brushed hers, forcing sudden heat into her cheeks, and a strange, undefinable embarrassment at the loss of control, something that only worsened when he casually slipped a large, dry palm beneath hers, threaded his fingers between hers and then closed them, locking their hands.

The touch captured her attention entirely, so only belatedly did she realize he was jeopardizing her manicure. She glanced downward and saw her nails were fine just as he leaned closer, his drawl sounding slow and easy, right next to her ear. "Hey there, Edie, sweetie."

Edie sweetie? Had her sister's relationship with Cash really progressed to pet names? Or was he simply playing to the cameras? Either way, his breath sent a shiver down her spine. Vaguely, Marley was aware that Trevor was interviewing the other couples, but she couldn't concentrate. Cash was better looking than she remembered. So big and muscular.

With bunched-up thighs and biceps that said he could easily lift twice her weight in the gym. It was almost enough to make Marley second-guess her motivations. But no...all she'd wanted was to make sure he meant Edie no harm....

But God, he was gorgeous. Oh, just a moment ago, she'd thought she had to go through with this so as not to jeopardize Edie's relationship with the Dardens and *Celebrity Weddings,* not to mention her reputation with the American public. But now, she realized she'd better come clean fast. She simply couldn't spend a week on hot dates with a man this sexy, whom she didn't trust....

"We know you're the lucky gal who's planning the upcoming wedding of hockey star Lorenzo Santini and hotel heiress Julia Darden. Isn't that right, Edie?"

The blood drained from her face. What if her sister's meeting with the Dardens was over—and she'd tuned in to the show? This really wasn't a sixth grade class where she and Edie could trade places as a joke. This was national TV.

"As you mentioned, Trevor," she found herself responding, her voice shaking just a little in a way she hoped no one noticed, "I'm a wedding planner." There. She'd just said a sentence to thousands of viewers, maybe millions. Amazing. She felt suddenly breathless. Electrified. Or maybe that was just from the way Cash Champagne was starting to stroke her hand, as if hell-bent on showing the public how hot they were together.

Marley just hated that her palm had begun sweating in Cash's. His was bone dry, as if he were on TV every night of his life. "I'd also like to talk about my sister," Marley managed to add, feeling only a twinge of guilt. After all, she might be able to pick up some clients. "Her name's Marley...and, uh, she's doing a wonderful job, working as Julia Darden's personal fitness trainer."

Now she knew Edie was going to kill her. It was bad enough to impersonate your twin, but she'd just stooped to using the opportunity to promote herself. Brazen hussy, she thought, but forced herself to continue. "Previously, Marley owned a wonderful fitness club called Fancy Abs, and she's currently shopping for a location for her new venture." It wasn't strictly true, since she still didn't have the money to do so, but maybe someone with an inexpensive rental property would see her on TV and call....

"It's great of you to give your sister such a glowing recommendation!" exclaimed Trevor. "No sibling rivalry there. You've shown just the kind of generosity that endears a contestant to our viewers."

Great. Really, it was Edie who deserved all the credit. She'd hooked Marley up with the Darden wedding and then introduced her to Emma Goldstein. That had led to Marley's writing a fitness column for *Celebrity Weddings*. So far, Marley had written Honed Honeymoon, Sex Muscles and Shapely Mates.

Feeling guilty, Marley hazarded her first glance toward Cash's dark, smoldering eyes and said, "Uh, look, Trevor...I'm not really sure Cash and I should be on this show."

Trevor only laughed. A quick glance at Cash showed her that he'd taken the news in stride. As soon as they got out of here, she'd explain everything.

Staring into the camera, Trevor winked knowingly. "We've got a female with cold feet. And what's our studio audience have to say about that?"

Bleeps and horns sounded as the audience pushed buttons on the armrests of their seats. A ding sounded. Then Trevor said, "Go, Edie! You and your date have been voted our underdog couple! If you win, your cash prize doubles. That means one-hundred thousand dollars for you and Cash!"

Marley's jaw slackened. Edie had said there was a cash prize, but nothing that hefty. Her first thought was that she could comfortably rent the space she needed to put Fancy Abs back in business. She wouldn't call it Fancy Abs, of course, since that era of her life, which had included Chris, was over. Her second thought was that she could never survive a week of dream dates with any man, much less Cash Champagne, at least not without having sex, which she'd foregone for a year now. And even if she could, the wedding curse would continue to wreak havoc with her future....

But what was she thinking? she chastised herself. She had to get off this show; otherwise, Edie was going to disown her as a sister.

"Really," Marley protested. "I've had second thoughts. I know it's unusual, but it would be great if you could call back the alternates. Anyone backstage will tell you I was trying to cancel. I really don't think…"

Trevor bellowed, "What does the studio audience say?"

The crowd punched buttons again. Another ding sounded, and Trevor shouted, "Double underdog!

These are two-time losers. She says she doesn't want to dream-date this man, studio audience! It's a tough sell. If these two win, the prize is now set at two-hundred thousand dollars for Cash and Edie!"

Marley was definitely weakening. But she was pretty sure the dream dates involved a lot of music, flowers and dressing up in fancy gowns provided by the studio, all romantic things Marley had shut the door on—for life. "That's an awful lot of money, Trevor, but I don't think…"

"Cash," Trevor interrupted. "You're a southern gentleman. Can you convince your date to help you win this pot of gold?"

Marley's already stuttering heart missed another beat as Cash sent the camera a devastating smile. He really was gorgeous, with tanned, reddish-chestnut skin, black hair that swept from his face like midnight, and eyes that promised he'd be scrumptious in bed, even if Edie had claimed it was false advertising.

"Why, Trevor," Cash drawled, "I can be quite persuasive with the ladies."

Persuasive? Oh no! Surely he didn't mean…

Marley watched in horror as Cash slowly rose to his feet, dressed in well-worn jeans that lovingly wrapped around his sculpted thighs, pointy-toed western boots and a sport coat the tawny color of a fawn. Turning, he gave the camera his delicious-looking backside, then placed sun-bronzed hands on the armrests of Marley's chair and hunkered down to eye level.

Ever so slowly, he ducked his head another notch. Her breath caught. So did his. Then he leaned another fraction and feathered his mouth across hers, offering a satisfied, smacking sound that Marley couldn't help but remember was reverberating over all the airwaves in America.

And then everything went black for just a heartbeat.

Fluttering her eyes, she wondered what had happened. Maybe she'd swooned. Her already woozy head swam, and even though her eyes were shut, the light seemed to shimmer as if she were walking through a desert under a hot sun. Vaguely, she was hoping Edie wasn't watching this, but she could almost hear Edie's phone ringing, and their mother's excited voice saying, "I know you're not there, Edie. I just wanted you to know that Daddy and I are watching you on TV right now! I know you said you weren't experiencing any sparks with your new fellow, but that's not what I'm seeing!"

Or what her sister was feeling. Molten heat had raced through her veins, zipping through her bloodstream, and she could only thank heaven that her feet were enclosed in Edie's painful high heels, so no one could see the unnatural angle at which her toes had curled.

As Cash drew back, the studio audience took in her stunned expression and screamed with delight, and then Trevor said, "Well, folks, it sure looks as if Edie's decided to be on our show!"

2

BE ON THE SHOW? After that kiss? No way, Marley thought, ripping the microphone from the lapel of the too-short suit when the cameras stopped rolling. The wool was making her legs itch so badly that she'd wanted to claw her thighs throughout the show, and now, since she'd gulped all that water, she was desperate to find a ladies' room.

Thankfully, the ridiculously frilly, high-collared blouse beneath the jacket had saved her torso from breaking into hives. Between the pancake foundation someone had applied during a commercial break, the candy-apple blusher and eye shadow better suited to a Hollywood diva, the makeup people who'd been manhandling her since she'd arrived had done a real number on her. Cash was just lucky she hadn't strong-armed him to the ground! After all, she had taught female self-defense courses at Fancy Abs. Of course Cash didn't know that because he thought she was Edie....

Yanking down the skirt as she stood, Marley prayed she'd kept her legs together during the show. Not that her panties, which were the only thing she was wearing that belonged to her, weren't decent. Unlike her twin's silk thongs, hers were of high-waisted cotton, bought two pairs for a dollar on the street in Chinatown. Careful not to make eye contact, she brushed past Cash, and then beelined toward an Exit sign over the door to the hallway, through which Trevor Milane had just vanished.

If only she could erase the memory of the past hour! Maybe she could just clunk herself on the head, she thought dryly as she hightailed after Trevor, and induce amnesia. Yes...she would refuse to dwell on the swollen feeling of her lips and the unwanted bereft sensation left in the wake of Cash's kiss, not to mention the undeniable pang solicited by the absence of his mouth, or the weightless, falling feeling she'd been sure she'd never experience again.

"Oh, this is not good," Marley whispered nervously. The last time she'd had this swooning feeling, her ex had been kissing her goodbye as she'd left for work. Or so she'd thought. Eleven hours later, she'd found the note that said he'd kissed her goodbye— forever. After taking the money from their joint accounts, he'd left for Key West to fulfill his lifelong ambition of living on a houseboat, a dream he'd somehow failed to mention to Marley before.

Still eyeing the Exit sign, she reminded herself that what Cash had forced her to experience was a mere bodily response to male stimuli. Cash's lips had landed on hers, and sure, she'd shuddered. Her belly had warmed, her blood had quickened, her thighs had squeezed together and her breasts had tightened. But it meant nothing. This New Year's, she'd sworn off men, but if a man did certain things, healthy women were bound to feel certain other things. Dabbing her upper lip, Marley wished hot sweats wasn't one of them.

Fortunately, she was mature. Her divorce had left her hardened and more worldly. Men's kisses could affect her body now, but not her mind. Never again would she let physical experiences sway her good judgment. Sure, immediately after Cash had kissed her, she'd *said* she'd remain on the show. And sure, to the viewers of America, it might have *looked* as if Cash had persuaded her with one stupid kiss.

But Marley had the power. She could easily have wrestled Cash to the floor with a headlock. Or kneed his groin. Oh, she really didn't trust him. He was too pretty, superficial and slick. With those prominent cheekbones, thick black hair and straight nose, he looked like a model or a rock star. He wasn't Marley's type, and besides, he was her sister's boyfriend, at least technically. And yes, maybe the word *boyfriend* was strong. Which was to the point. Marley had suspected this man's motives. She couldn't put her finger on it, but she could tell Cash had some ulterior reason for dating Edie….

Barreling through the door, she entered the long hallway she'd traversed earlier, her legs teetering. Why she couldn't walk in Edie's high heels, she'd never know. Snowboarding was her favorite pastime, and she in-line skating down the West Side Highway at speeds that beat city traffic.

Run, run, run, her mind was screaming. But her ankles were wobbling. The stilettos were catching on the thick pile of the carpet. Unfortunately, most of the office doors were shut, and she needed to talk to Trevor. He'd know how to rectify this situation. She thought she'd glimpsed his nameplate at the far end of the hallway. She had to get off the show. There was no other alternative after that...

Kiss.

Her throat closed at the thought of the lip-lock that had made her workouts seem tame. Her head swam, and vaguely, she wondered if it had really been a year since she'd had sex. Heat had burned off her as Cash mushed his lips to hers, and she figured she must have lost at least a pound, maybe two. It had definitely been a calorie-burning sizzler. Even now, she could see those suntanned fingers curling around the armrests of her seat, trapping her. Just as she'd gasped, the scent of his skin had tunneled to her lungs, and a heartbeat later, the silken tip of his tongue had teased open her lips, wetting them....

But who was he, really? He'd scarcely touched Edie, which was one reason Marley didn't trust him. Face it, men craved sex like air, and so Cash's hands-off policy with Marley's twin was suspicious. And he didn't live in New York. Oh, he'd *said* he was from New Orleans, and he'd *said* he was helping a friend open a club, but Marley was convinced that the whole story wouldn't hold water, not if she played armchair detective, made a few phone calls and checked him out. Maybe she'd do just that....

Suddenly, she squealed. "Ouch!" He'd grabbed her from behind, closing his fingers around her upper arm. "Let me go, Cash."

"How'd you know it was me?"

Yeah, right. She'd smelled the clean male scent of him and heard the soft brush of his boot heels on the carpet. Somehow, she couldn't force herself to turn around and face him, not yet. No heat in the man's kisses? What had her twin been talking about? His every pore was leaking testosterone. "That's the other thing," Marley muttered hotly, hardly caring that she was continuing a monologue she'd been having in her head.

"What's that?"

Wrenching her arm away, she whirled to face him. "I guess the rumors about southern men are true."

His laugh shouldn't have been annoying, but it was. "Which rumor? That we kiss to beat the band?"

"No, the rumor about having your way with women, regardless of their feelings. You have a pretty high opinion of yourself."

"I hadn't even started talking about myself yet." Cash's dark eyes twinkled with amusement. "Just my kisses."

"They might not fly so well in Yankee territory," she returned sweetly in her best southern accent, rapidly batting her eyelashes, a move that didn't come naturally.

"I don't see why we need to make this a North-South issue, since the Civil War was over a long time ago."

"Ah. But was it really civil?"

"No war is," he agreed.

Fortunately, she'd made it halfway to Trevor's office, and now she reminded herself that, in just a moment, she'd be released from her obligation to the show, at least if she were lucky. Surely, they could start over tomorrow with the alternates. "Look. This isn't what you think."

The eyes drifting down every inch of her didn't look convinced, but they did look curious. "No?"

This would shake him up. "I'm not Edie."

She almost smiled, since she'd clearly unsettled him. Finally. With satisfaction, she watched his calm, cool, collected demeanor change, and she felt glad she was wearing Edie's high heels. Now that she was standing still, the shoes made her tall enough to meet his liquid eyes.

As the seconds ticked on, however, she got uncomfortable again. She became overly conscious of people crowding into the hallway, the flicker of fluorescent lights and the shortness of her own breath. She became aware of other things, too, which she'd have preferred to ignore, such as how his well-worn jeans clung to lean hips and snuggled around the unmistakable rise beneath his zipper. The other male contestants had worn suits, but Cash had somehow stopped the reality-show staff from wrestling him out of his beloved jeans. She glanced around. Where were the other contestants, anyway? Had they exited by another doorway? And why wasn't he saying anything?

When he finally did, he said, "You're not Edie?"

She hated to disappoint him. Feeling a twinge of guilt, she rushed on. "Uh…I know I look like her tonight. I mean, with the blown-out hair and makeup." She was even wearing panty hose. "But…" In midsentence, her mouth went dry again. He really was incredibly good-looking. Somehow, she managed to repeat, "Uh…no, I'm not Edie."

He said the last thing expected. "Uh…no shit, Marley."

Her heart fluttered. "You *knew?*" Oh, this made everything so much worse.

"Uh…yeah."

She squinted. "So, why did you look surprised?"

"Uh…I thought you knew that *I knew* that you weren't…" His voice trailed off.

At what exact point had he known? She had to ask. "When? Before or after?" *The kiss.*

He rubbed a jaw that was turning dark with five-o'clock stubble, his equally dark eyebrows knitting together. "I suspected all along," he said in a slow drawl. "But I wasn't sure until you kissed me. Let's just say…you two don't kiss alike."

"TMI," she managed to say, not about to encourage anything more about her sister's kissing habits.

"TMI?"

"Too much information."

"You asked me," he pointed out.

"I didn't kiss you, though. You kissed me." Big difference. How could men be so deluded? Marley hated to generalize, but it wasn't just Cash who seemed too full of himself. Lots of men overestimated their prowess. Marley was hardly the first woman to notice, either. History was full of astute women who had managed to pick up on this. "I did nothing," she clarified, hoping he understood. "I sat there in stunned silence."

Those inky eyes, so alive with shadow, widened. "Really?"

Why didn't he seem to believe her? "Just now—" Marley jerked her thumb back toward the studio. "When *you* kissed *me*," she continued, placing correct emphasis on the pronouns, "my mouth dropped open in shock. Maybe you saw more into that than it really was, Cash."

"Maybe so," he said, the words running together like molasses, his lips pursing pensively, "and since I pride myself on paying close attention, Marley, I have to apologize. I don't know what confused me more, the way you flung your arms around my neck, or the way you went at me with all that tongue action."

"Do men really say things like this?" she muttered. "Tongue action?"

He looked like he was fighting a smile. "Apparently, some do."

Had she used her tongue? *Had* she wrapped her arms around his neck? Shutting her eyes briefly, she tried to remember, but she drew a blank. Surely, he was wrong. She'd remember if she'd kissed him back. "Look," she began diplomatically, opening her eyes. "On this issue, let's agree to disagree. Apparently, we each have our own version."

Before he could contradict her, she quickly cleared her throat. "And my being on the show wasn't intentional," she plunged on. "Edie had nothing to do with it. She doesn't even know. She asked me to come here, but not to be on the show with you. I mean, it's not like we were trading places with each other, the way we did when we were kids." He was looking at her expectantly, so she added, "It's a long story...."

"I've got all night."

"Well, I don't," she assured quickly.

"If you're in a hurry, I'm all ears."

Still trying to ignore the fact that they'd kissed at all, much less on national television, she took a deep breath and said, "Edie's been trying to call you all day." She tried to keep the accusation from her tone, but still, if Cash had made himself available to his own girlfriend, none of this would have happened. "She said you disappeared, but she wanted you to know she had second thoughts about being on the show."

"She couldn't come?"

"She got hung up." When he didn't look convinced, she added, "Really. She had to pick up ring designs from Bridget before she met the Dardens for a wedding-planning meeting."

"So she sent you?"

"Sent would be strong," Marley corrected, hardly about to divulge her own plans to interrogate him. "She *asked* and I agreed." She wouldn't have it implied that she took orders from Edie. "I tried to call your hotel and your cell phone, but there was no answer. I came here to leave a message, but one thing led to another. The male and female contestants were separated," she explained, "and before I could stop them, the staff pushed me into the green room."

"Even after you said you wanted off the show?"

She nodded. "I was trying to make them stop putting on makeup…"

He looked at her as if noticing the eye shadow for the first time. "Understandable."

"And nails." She held up blood-red talons. "They seemed to think lots of color would play well for the camera—" Pausing, she scrutinized him. "I can see now that only women were targeted, and the men were spared."

Cash deadpanned. "You don't like my blow-dry?"

"You even got to wear jeans."

"They said I had cowboy appeal."

"Cowboy appeal?"

He shrugged. "The boots."

"The only thing about me they liked was Edie's hairdo." Puffing her cheeks, she realized Cash's eyes had locked on to hers. Whew. Some eyes. How come Edie hadn't responded to this guy? Suddenly, everything went still. She registered the people milling around them and the fact that, despite the crowd, she felt as if she were alone with him.

"I like you better in sweatpants."

Marley wished he hadn't said it. "You like sweatpants?"

"Not so much as the sports bras and ripped midriffs that go with them."

"Hmm." This was the guy whom Edie had sworn lacked testosterone? Granted, Marley tried to stay out of her sister's love life, which was easy, since it was virtually nonexistent, but still, she'd gotten roped into at least one conversation about Cash's supposed deficiencies. Definitely, she had to draw some very firm boundaries here. "Well, you've probably noticed that, uh, I'm not very available."

"You're abrupt," he agreed, a slow, sexy smile saying he didn't mind in the least. "Downright rude the day I offered you a ride."

"It's nothing personal," she assured.

"How is rudeness not personal?"

"I was trying to be discouraging," she corrected. "Not rude." She just wished he weren't studying her with eyes hot enough to melt glaciers.

"So, Edie wanted off the show?" He really did look disappointed.

"I'm sorry, but it's nothing personal. She just

thought the better of it. Honestly, I think she re-membered the wedding curse and just got a case of jitters. You do know about the family curse, don't you?"

"Not much. Maybe you can tell me more."

Not in this lifetime. "Uh…maybe. But right now, we have a lot of other things on our plate, right? I do think we can work this out. Trevor Milane will know what to do. I was just headed to his office…." She flashed an insincere smile, hardly able to muster a genuine one, not when her nostrils were filled with his enticing male scent, and his hard, hot body was this close. "Why don't you come along?"

Deciding not to prolong the conversation—or agony—she turned on one of Edie's high heels and wobbled down the hallway, not surprised to feel Cash close behind. "Mr. Milane," she said when she reached his office.

Seated at his desk, he looked up. "Yes?"

When she felt a jolt of electricity behind her, she realized Cash's chest had brushed her back, and she tried to ignore how her heart jump-started. "I can't be on *Rate the Dates*. I've been trying to explain this ever since I got here. Who can I talk to?"

"Of course you're on the show," Trevor soothed, rising and circling his desk. "I know you're a bundle of nerves. But our staff is trained to handle jitters."

"I don't have jitters," Marley corrected. He was making her sound like the proverbial neurotic female.

"Everything will be fine, Edie," Trevor assured.

"Really?" she managed to say dryly. Just hearing people address her by her sister's name was driving her crazy. And even though it wasn't the end of January yet, a man was already threatening her New Year's resolution never to have sex again. She was going to live as a single, rebuilding her business, making her own money and traveling. No man would destroy the fruits of her labors again.

"Edie—" Trevor cooed the name as if she were an invalid. One headlock, Marley thought silently, and that calculating smile would vanish from Trevor Milane's face. But then, as her Granny Ginny always said, "A woman catches more flies with honey," so she plastered a smile on her face, reminding herself that Trevor had the power right now. If anybody could get her off the show, it was probably him.

"You're about to meet the videographer who'll be taping your dates all week," he was saying. "His name's Vinny Marcel, and as soon as he arrives, we'll get started."

"Things aren't as they appear," Marley began again.

"No," Trevor agreed slowly, his smile thinning. "They aren't." She watched as he opened a drawer to his desk and withdrew a document. "You signed this?"

"I…thought I was signing for the bottled water," she said. "You know," she explained, "the way you sign for food and drinks at a hotel."

"This is NBC. Do you really think we'd make contestants pay for water?"

Well…she had thought it a bit ungracious. "I wasn't sure."

"Well, we don't."

"Uh-oh. That's not a contract, is it?"

Just as he nodded, Marley got near enough for her eyes to settle on the dotted line where she'd signed Edie's name. "But I didn't know what it was…."

Wasn't there some law that protected people who were forced to sign legal documents under duress?

"You know now, Edie," Trevor said succinctly.

It was the wrong time for a bearded man with a video camera to appear in the doorway. "Cash and Edie," he said, introducing himself with a wide grin, "I'm Vinny Marcel, your videographer. Are we ready to rock?"

"Rock?" Marley whispered softly. What lower level of hell had she just stumbled into? Was she really going to be videotaped for a week, while some southern hunk stuck to her like glue?

She was actually thankful when she felt Cash's palm glide across her back. The fingers settled at the small of her spine, and although they exerted only the slightest pressure, the touch sent shivers through her body. So did his lips, which connected with her ear.

Softly, so only she could hear, he whispered in a drawl that melted each inch of her, "My truck's in the parking garage next door. What say, we excuse ourselves by saying we're going to the little boys' and girls' rooms, respectively—and then we'll just make a run for it, Marley?"

It was another reminder that she really did want to find a ladies' room. Right before she whispered, "Okay," a wave of fear shot through her system, and it took her a second to properly identify its source: against all her better judgment, she was actually starting to like this man.

3

ONCE HE WAS INSIDE Marley's apartment, Cash thought maybe there was some credence to the Benning wedding curse, since the Fates had definitely thrown a wrench into his plans.

"I have to wash off this makeup and change." Marley quickly shrugged out of the fur coat and tossed it over the back of a chair. "I don't know how Edie stands these clothes."

Cash wasn't partial to Edie's stylistic choices, either. "Take your time."

As she headed toward a chest of drawers, Cash tried not to notice how easily her well-honed body moved, with grace and economy. Taking off his coat, he tossed it on top of the fur and glanced around, wishing he didn't feel quite so curious about Marley's lifestyle. He'd meant to date a Benning, for his own reasons; actually becoming attracted to one of the women wasn't supposed to be in the cards.

Marley's door had opened onto a large, airy room overlooking the Hudson River and Brooklyn Promenade. It was a studio, but had a bedroom alcove Marley was using as a combination sitting room-office. As she pulled a pair of sweats from the drawer, and a top that would unfortunately cover more of her than the midriffs she'd worn the couple times he'd glimpsed her, he fought disappointment. He'd liked the skimpier clothes. He missed the way her hair usually looked, too, with wild blond waves drawn into a ponytail. Curls usually fell into her smoky blue eyes, the only feature she shared with her supposedly look-alike twin.

She shot him a wary glance. "Help yourself to anything in the fridge."

"Do you happen to have a beer?"

"Only rice milk and carrot juice."

"I think I'll pass, but thanks."

She actually laughed, and he was glad to hear it, since it helped break the tension. "Fooled you. I've got Bass Ale and Moosehead. Take your pick. And feel free to fold the futon."

"Fold the futon?"

"What is this? A living version of the old joke?"

"What old joke?"

"If you want to get rid of a guy, tell him to do housework."

"Do you want to get rid of me?"

She didn't miss a beat. "Obviously."

He liked that she was sharp, fast on her feet. Her angry edge and guarded tone made for easy banter. "I don't mind folding the futon," he replied, unable to ignore how she kept checking him out. No, Marley Benning was just as attracted to him as he was to her, and she didn't hide it nearly as well as she thought.

She didn't sound convinced. "Hmm."

But the mother who'd raised Cash single-handedly had been a maid, so he was no stranger to cleaning. He had fond memories of following her around as a kid, and he associated scents of soap with the person in his life who'd loved him best, even if he kept his own home on the sloppy side.

"You'll have to fold the futon if you want to sit."

"No problem." He took another look around, his gaze settling on a coffee table strewn with empty fast-food bags, rolled magazines and self-help books stamped with coffee rings. "It looks like the scene they always have in movies about depressed single women," he couldn't help but tease.

"Don't tell me you watch movies like *Bridget Jones' Diary*."

"Are you kidding?" he joked. "It was a lot better than poker with the guys, or Monday night football."

"Somehow, I don't believe you." She actually smiled. "I'm still working on the overall effect. I think I need some more empty Chinese takeout cartons."

"Maybe some overdue videos," he added helpfully. "And unpaid bills. You might even add a big, unopened box of condoms, just to look hopeful." On the back of her door, she'd hung a dartboard with a man's picture skewered to the bull's eye. "The ex?"

Her laughter deepened to a sexy, throaty sound that was remarkably unlike her sister's airy chuckles. Cash was very glad her mood seemed to have improved. Maybe it was due to how deftly they'd escaped the videographer or the novelty of their ride to Brooklyn. Marley had informed Cash that she'd never been in a truck before, only cars and trains, and because the traffic had been so heavy, they hadn't done much talking.

"Chris Lang," she clarified after a moment, then

she smirked at Cash. "You guessed who it was right off the bat. You're smarter than you look."

"You make me feel so special," he returned dryly, lifting a book from the table called *Life After Divorce*, the cover of which had been splashed with morning cereal. Raising an eyebrow in her direction, he added, "Should I disinfect anything?"

"Probably," she warned darkly as she headed for the bathroom, "but only if you don't want to pick up dread diseases. But don't feel obligated. It's your call."

He decided he kind of liked the place. Overly organized dwellings like Edie's made him nervous. He couldn't relax in them. Still, he couldn't help but ask, "You're sure you and Edie are sisters?"

"Rumor has it the culprit was the postman," Marley assured right before the bathroom door swung shut.

He stared at it a moment, his chest growing tight as he imagined her taking off the suit jacket and blouse. He'd never forget the first time he'd seen her in the dingy East Village comedy club. She'd taken his breath away, which was why he'd been glad she was leaving the club early. He'd wound up flirting with her less-interesting twin, and he'd figured that way, once he'd gotten what he wanted from a relationship with a Benning, it would be easier to break things off....

Unfortunately, he'd seen Marley again a few days before Christmas, bounding into Big Apple Brides, fresh from one of her hours-long jogs along the newly landscaped West Side Highway running track.

"Edie?" she'd called, her voice husky with the winter air. "You said you didn't have clients coming this afternoon, so I stopped by. I've got to borrow some clothes before I go back to Brooklyn. It started snowing and I got soaked, and Mom wants me to stay in the city for dinner."

He'd been in the conference room with Edie, and his heart had missed a beat as he'd watched through the door. Marley had yanked off a cap, releasing tangled blond hair that fell around her reddened cheeks. And then she'd smiled. She'd looked so free, self-possessed and strong that excitement had surged inside him. Especially when she'd kept undressing, stripping off outerwear, tossing aside snow-wet clothes until she was down to a midriff worn over a sports bra and spandex leggings.

A moment later, when she'd entered the conference room, and Edie had reintroduced them, rehashing their first meeting at the club, he'd been both annoyed and intrigued to see Marley's expression become guarded. Her blue eyes had flashed hot with desire, turned the dark color of a bayou sky before a storm, then narrowed into an attitude of wary distrust.

It was unsettling. As if she had seen right through him. Surely it was only his imagination, but she'd seemed to guess his hidden agenda. His every secret seemed exposed, from the misspent youth he'd enjoyed before his mama got sick, to all the drinking, carousing and hot sex in his truck bed with women who'd giggled under the stars with him on sultry bayou nights. Maybe Marley had even guessed that he'd nearly killed a man.

But then Cash figured it was just his guilty conscience talking. At most, Marley had felt a dangerous undercurrent she couldn't define, mixed with a healthy dose of physical attraction for him. Now

Cash contemplated his next move. Maybe Edie hadn't seen the kiss on TV. According to Marley, she'd had a meeting tonight. So, what next?

Finally, he decided that one Benning sister was as good as another. If Edie had asked Marley to find him and cancel the appearance on *Rate the Dates*, it was probably over between them, something about which he felt only relief. There was no chemistry between them, which had made their few necessary kisses nearly unbearable. But with Marley...

Cutting off the thought, he continued surveying her space, now wishing it had better acoustics or that she'd turned on music, since he could swear he'd heard her skirt hit the floor. Her perfume had tempted him during the ride across the Brooklyn Bridge, too, filling the cramped cab of his truck. The kiss, though...well, that had grabbed him, lifted him off his feet and shaken him. He'd even forgotten they were on TV. The swirl of her tongue—a response she seemed anxious to deny—had swept inside him, whisking his sex drive as if he'd been caught in the eye of a tornado.

And now Marley Benning was naked.

Albeit on the other side of the closed bathroom door. He felt a sudden urge to leave. Instead, he took a deep breath and headed as far away from the bathroom as he could get, which meant the kitchenette. Raising his voice, he called, "You want a beer?"

"Sure. Bass."

Bringing the drinks back to the living room, he folded the futon, and then scrutinized the articles she'd written for *Celebrity Weddings*, which were pinned to a bulletin board. "Don't say a word," she begged, raising a staying hand as she swept into the room.

Even though she hadn't removed the red nail polish, she looked more like herself, wearing a soft, cuddly-looking outfit of gray sweats and a sloppy hooded T-shirt. Quickly, he knocked back a swallow of beer, glad for the splash of cold to the back of his throat and the warmth that followed. Then he smiled. "You have a way with words. Honed Honeymoon shows real flair."

She rolled her eyes. "I'm lucky to get the work. It was nice of Edie to introduce me to Emma. She's the writer covering the Darden wedding." Marley paused. "Well…you probably know that."

He did. "Edie mentioned that coaching brides-to-be about physical fitness wasn't your first love," he said with a hint of a smile. "Uh…she said your ex took all your money, and you had to close your business. You're much more into defense training for women and bodybuilding." He paused. "You also made a New Year's resolution to never become involved with a man again."

She swallowed a sip of beer, her tongue darting out to lick any leftover drops. "She told you all that?"

He nodded. "Yeah. The depression led to your eating fast foods even though you and Chris had been vegans."

"I worked five years to build my business," she said defensively. "Nights. Weekends. Everything."

"Sorry," he said simply.

Seemingly giving up on trying to keep him at arm's length, she seated herself at the far end of the futon, drawing slender bare feet up beneath her, and she took another healthy swig of beer, heaving a worried sigh when he followed suit and sat beside her. "I never was as neat as Edie. But…"

Frowning, he considered the fast-food bags. "McDonalds?"

She took a deep breath. "Only when Burger King's not open." She hesitated, sighing deeply. "I can't believe Edie told you about my relationship with my husband."

"Not the whole thing," he assured. "Just the ending."

"Still…"

He shrugged. "It came up when she mentioned the wedding curse."

"Ah. So, she probably told you that Bridget applied to the *Guinness Book of World Records* for having survived the most bad dates in Manhattan, too."

"Yeah. But she never told me all the details, just that your Granny Ginny swears a curse was put on your family." It was something Edie had brought up right after one of their not-so-hot kisses. Now Cash couldn't help but think that the heat generated between him and Marley in the studio proved the curse wrong—not that he'd point it out….

"So, she told you Joe Benning's not our biological father?"

"She said your mother's first husband, your father, died shortly after you were born, and that the curse really comes from his side."

She bobbed her head. "My father died when Edie and I were three. Bridget was just a newborn. And my father's mother, our Granny Ginny," she clarified, "is visiting later this week from Florida. Given all that happened...with my marriage...well, I'm finally convinced that what she's said about the curse might be true." She sent him a wry smile, as if barely able to believe what she was saying.

Once more he thought of the kiss that had knocked him senseless. "Really," he found himself murmuring. "You don't seem cursed, Marley."

She eyed him. "You're an expert on curses?"

"Well, no," he admitted.

Shaking her head, she stared through the bay window, the apartment's best feature, into the liquid night. Neither had mentioned it yet, but it sure looked as if they were about to spend a week together, going on prearranged dates, designed to make them fall in love, and now he realized that her feelings about the family curse were playing into what was happening.

She did seem unsettled. And he wasn't sure how he wanted to broach their appearance on *Rate the Dates.* Should he appear glad about it? As if his motive were only the cash prize? Or angry, since she'd impersonated her sister?

Remaining silent, he followed her gaze. To the right, the impressive arches of the Brooklyn Bridge stretched into a black sky studded with stars, shining with the same kind of promise that *Rate the Dates* offered its contestants. City lights from Manhattan were swimming in a river of shimmering colors. Taking another sip of beer, she shot him a studious glance. "Usually, I really do only offer soy milk and juice," she admitted. "I get up at five in the morning. Run on a tight schedule until I fall into bed. I...I've gotten a little off track, which is why..."

Had she been about to apologize for the way she'd kissed him in the studio? He'd been sure her arms had looped around his neck. She—not he—had initiated that mind-blowing kiss. How was he supposed to handle this turn of events? "Edie said your husband took off to Florida," he said conversationally, buying time.

She nodded. "Chris and I dated two years in college, but after we got married, he changed. I think he felt tied down, especially when I started thinking about having kids. He took our money without warning. My business folded as a result, and I sold our condo in Queens to pay off debts, mostly his."

"You didn't go after him legally?"

"I couldn't."

So, she'd loved him. "I can respect that."

She shrugged. "He said he wanted to do something deeper with his life. More meaningful."

"What was deeper than loving you?" he asked, really wanting to know, but delivering the words in a stagy drawl that took the edge off the question, something that must have worked, since she laughed again.

"Living on a houseboat." Her eyes suddenly sparkled with wickedness, making them look less like blue storm clouds and a little more like crystal waters. "I told him I hoped he'd sink in his houseboat. Now, that would be."

Marley was the type to fall hard, but she'd get back up again. Leaning, he stretched out his legs, angling his body toward hers as he draped an arm along the back of the futon. "So, what are we going to do?"

Instead of responding, he suddenly shivered. "Cold?"

"A little," he admitted. "Coming from down south, I'm not used to the weather."

"The steam heat in this place is totally unpredictable. Here." She tossed him an end of an afghan.

As he drew it over his lap, their eyes met and, for a moment, they simply stared at each other. He became aware of the silence, the hitch of her breath. She was being more provocative than she could admit to herself, he decided. It wasn't his imagination. She'd circled his neck with her arms in the studio, pulling him down, so the impact of his mouth was hard. She'd wanted to feel him that way—his lips hot and crushing. In his arms, she'd felt hungry, eager. It had lasted only a minute, which meant not nearly long enough, and now he was thoroughly conscious of his desire to kiss her again.

Suddenly, his chest constricted. Vaguely, he wondered what he was doing here. It was wrong to use her this way. She was too pretty and hardworking. Determined and sassy. She'd pulled herself up by the bootstraps, only to be let down, and now he was risking playing with her emotions....

"Marley," he began.

"Hmm?"

He told himself to simply get up and leave. Maybe the lawyers who worked for him could get them both off the show. If she'd come clean about her identity, breaking the contract would be possible, even with a major corporation like NBC. He'd just say he'd only intended to be on the show with Edie. Instead, he fixed his gaze on hers, his voice dropping lower of its own accord, and he said, "I want to kiss you again."

His blood quickened as she leaned forward, placing her beer on the table. He thought she was freeing her hands so they could claim his neck once more, but when they didn't, he realized she was preparing to defend herself, instead. "I won't do anything you don't want me to," he said.

"You couldn't," she said. "I know self-defense."

Somehow, the idea of her wrestling him to the floor had its appeal. "So I heard."

"Even if I wanted to…it's not a good idea, Cash."

"Nothing fun ever is," he offered.

Her voice sounded strained. "Good point."

"We're going to be on TV," he found himself saying. "I mean, it's clear we can't get out of it…." His breath caught as he wondered if his lawyers would agree, then he let go of the thought, knowing he couldn't pass up the opportunity to get to know her.

"And you're suggesting we practice for the show?"

Turning toward her, scooting closer on the futon, he raked a slow finger down her cheek, exploring glowing skin that felt like velvet before tracing her lower lip. He couldn't believe she was actually letting him do this. Her eyes were unblinking, riveted on his face.

"I don't think…" she began again.

"Good," he murmured, silently cursing a situation that had brought him to a city he hated and hadn't visited for years. He was in Marley's apartment under false pretenses, too, and even though he didn't want to, he craved her. Biting back a curse, he wondered why her fool sister hadn't shown up in the studio, as planned. He felt nothing for Edie. Oh, she was a nice person, but her body left him cold. There had been none of the spark he felt right now. How could women who were supposedly identical have such opposite effects?

"Don't think," he found himself murmuring. "Thinking gets in the way."

"I made a New Year's resolution not to…"

"I just want to remind you of what you're missing," he said, the air leaving his lungs. His chest was tight as he angled his head farther down, stopping just shy of a touch of their lips. No, he wouldn't kiss her yet. He'd enjoy the warmth of her breath, the sweet mint scent. Her breath hitched, catching in her throat, and he imagined her blood quickening, dancing with awareness.

"We're all alone now," he whispered, leaning another harrowing inch toward her mouth. He felt her shudder as his lips brushed softly across hers. He nibbled them, the motion feathery, and all at once, his groin tightened almost painfully with need, driving him to deepen the sensation, using both lips, his tongue, kissing her deeply, until he drew back, thinking of so many other things they could do tonight, murmuring, "America's not watching now…"

It was the wrong time for a loud knock to sound.

Startled, her lips looking red and bruised, Marley flinched, leaning backward. Just as surprised, he jerked his head toward the door, his jaw slackening. He couldn't believe the timing. "How'd they get into your building? I saw a downstairs buzzer."

Tossing off the afghan and looking relieved, as if she'd been under a sorcerer's spell and had come to her senses, Marley rose and moved toward the door. "It's someone I know. The buzzer breaks all the time, so my friends have keys to the lobby door. Stretching on her toes, she peered through the peephole, then announced in an ominous tone, made husky by his kiss, "Edie."

"Great," he managed to say.

After twisting three dead bolts, Marley lifted off a chain, swung open the door, and Edie Benning marched inside, looking fit to kill.

"LET ME GUESS," said Marley, silently praying her sister would cut her a break. "You saw the show?"

"I have a TV," Edie announced primly, in the same knowing tone people used when they said, *I have eyes*. "What's going on here?"

"Nothing's going on," Marley assured.

With exaggerated motions, Edie shut the door behind her, then spun toward the living room again, making the hem of a full-skirted black coat swish around her calves. Ever so slowly, as if barely able to contain her fury, she removed a matching black hat, untied a scarf, and one by one, removed her gloves, tapping them against her side to remove wrinkles before neatly folding and pocketing them.

"We can explain," Marley said quickly. She glanced toward the futon, and as Cash rose, she wished he didn't look quite so guilty. Or aroused, with his eyes smoky and his lips damp. Even worse, when she glimpsed herself in a mirror, she was stunned to see her disheveled hair, blurry eyes and lips the ruby color of her nails.

Unbuttoning her coat, Edie exposed a trim gray suit. Her eyes, which had been scanning the apartment, settled on the beer bottles and afghan. Yes, things looked incredibly cozy, Marley realized.

"Having a nightcap?" Before either Cash or Marley could speak, Edie continued, "Before you say a word to me, Cash, I want to tell you—"

Interrupting herself, Edie gasped. Eyes the same blue as Marley's turned a shade darker, until they seemed like rain clouds. Not a good sign. "What's wrong now?" Marley asked worriedly.

"I can't believe you," Edie muttered.

That makes two of us, Marley thought. Had she really let Cash kiss her again? Had she gone nuts? Only hours ago, she'd gone to great lengths to dress as her twin for the purpose of interrogating him. Now she'd fallen into his arms like a woman under a magician's spell. Why on earth hadn't she and Cash gone to Big Apple Brides instead of coming to her apartment?

But it had seemed so...well, *natural* for her and Cash to come here and decide what to do next. As Edie snatched her fur from beneath Cash's coat on the chair, then strode toward the bathroom, Marley fought to squelch another wave of guilt. "Really," she called. "We were just about to call you. Because you had a meeting, it never even occurred to me that you'd be home. I didn't think you'd watch the show...."

"Well, I did." She glanced over her shoulder. "And so did Mom and Dad."

"Did they realize it was me?"

"Yes. The switcheroo might work on most of America, but our folks are never going to be fooled." Edie closed the bathroom door behind her.

Marley swallowed hard. She'd heard how lackluster Edie's few kisses with Cash had been, but Edie and their parents had witnessed the explosive passion she'd shared with Cash. Somehow, the thought was unsettling. Her parents knew she kissed on dates, of course, but she didn't really want them witnessing such things.

"I feel bad about this, Edie, I really do," Marley sputtered, her heart squeezing tightly. She and Edie might be black and white in terms of stylistic choices, but they were still twins and they loved each other. Toying anxiously with the string tie to her sweatpants, she stared toward the bathroom door, waiting for Edie to reappear.

"I did what you asked, Edie," she continued. "You know I didn't really want to go to the studio. I said no at first."

"At first, but then you were easily talked into it."

Marley sent Cash a nervous glance, then she lunged into the account she'd given him earlier, describing once more how she'd been railroaded onto the set and accidently signed a contract. "I thought I was signing for bottled water," she explained. Deciding that a white lie wouldn't hurt, she continued, "It wasn't my idea to wear my hair the way you do yours, either, but they insisted on blow-drying it. Uh…all the TV people thought your hairstyle was much more becoming…."

Edie came from the bathroom, still clutching the fur coat while shaking wrinkles from the suit. "Wild animals could nest in your hair, Marley."

"So true," Marley agreed, ignoring the unbidden shudder that rippled through her as she imagined how Cash's fingers had felt a moment ago, traipsing against her scalp. Edie's penetrating gaze drew her from the fantasy.

After carefully draping the suit over her arm, Edie held up her other hand as if she were expecting to stop heavy traffic. "You're my sister," she said with exaggerated calm. "We grew up in the same apartment. We have the same parents. But when I see things such as this..." Edie stared at the suit, her eyes nearly closing as she shook her head. "I got this suit at Barneys, Marley."

Marley was just glad that Edie was more upset over the suit than Cash. Men would come and go, but for her sister, Valentino reigned forever. "I went to the studio, just like you asked," Marley reiterated quickly, sensing Edie's growing calm. "But I wound up on the show—"

"The show I was supposed to be on!"

"You canceled," Marley protested, still nervously winding the sweatpant string around her finger.

"That didn't give you license to go on the air!"

"I didn't intentionally!"

"Or pretend to be me!"

"I had to," Marley countered. "To get in the studio." Telling Edie that she'd intentionally impersonated her would only make matters worse.

"You even promoted your own work!"

Marley flushed guiltily.

"And now you're going to win the cash prize, too," Edie concluded. "I could have used that money for my business."

"But you were canceling," Marley repeated. "And I didn't go on to get the money, either. Neither did Cash. I already told you how they strong-armed me."

Edie, pausing only long enough to shoot Cash a long look, returned her gaze to Marley. "I felt so sorry for you," she crooned. "Why, when I saw all those chains and shackles they wrapped around you, Marley..."

"Cash thought I was you," Marley quickly assured. Lowering her voice to a whisper she hoped Cash couldn't hear, she added, "and you were going to break up. You said it just wasn't happening...you know." In bed.

"I really did think she was you," Cash put in.

Edie softened. "Really?"

They both nodded, rapidly moving their heads up and down.

"Well, that doesn't change the situation," Edie continued after a moment.

"No, it doesn't," agreed Marley. "But I don't think we can get off the show now." Imploring eyes settled on her sister. "I really did try, sis. After we aired, I went straight to Trevor Milane, but I didn't want to tell them I wasn't you, since that might hurt your reputation with the Dardens and *Celebrity Weddings*."

Edie blew out a frustrated sigh.

"I have a solution," Cash said slowly. "You need money for your new business, Edie, so does Marley. So, since Marley and I can't get out of the contract, we might as well do our best. If Marley and I win, we'll split the money three ways."

He sounded so reasonable. And he didn't sound particularly upset that the focus of Edie's pique was the show, not him. Still...so much for Marley's resolve to avoid male contact. Now, she still wanted to interrogate Cash, but for her own reasons. She waited.

Finally Edie said, "I think I can live with this."

Impulsively, Marley reached and put her hand on

Edie's arm, brushing her fingers over the material of her sister's sleeve, which was still cool from the January night. "We probably won't win," she assured, pushing aside the admission that she and Cash really were about to embark on a week of dream dates. "I mean, we've already been chosen as the underdogs. But if we do, the prize is two-hundred thousand dollars. That's almost seventy thousand dollars each." She was still thinking of Cash's kiss on the futon, so Marley couldn't believe how practical she sounded. "That would be enough to rent a space. I could reopen a health club, and you could start building reserves."

Everything made sense. Besides, how bad could it be to date Cash just for a week? Marley watched Edie's mind whirling. She knew her sister like the back of her hand and could read each thought, as plain as day. Edie really had intended to quit seeing Cash. And she wanted the money, too, to help give Big Apple Brides a boost. Besides, after speaking with Trevor, it was clear to Marley that the contract was binding. Unfortunately, there was no way to fool herself into thinking that the money was her sole concern. Cash's two kisses had piqued her interest, and she might as well admit it…

"*Celebrity Weddings* did want me to go on the show," Edie conceded. "So, if you can continue to pretend you're me…"

"They'll be satisfied," Marley confirmed. "My daily routine can remain the same. My workouts with Julia are early in the morning, and *Rate the Dates* doesn't want contestants on the set until noon. Starting tomorrow, they said that's when they want us to arrive."

Edie considered. "Pete Shriver, Julia's bodyguard, wants you to give workouts at the estate now, for security reasons. He wants to send a car for you every morning."

Marley squinted. "Why?"

Edie plunged into an explanation, saying that Julia was receiving threatening letters and had been for some time. After she finished, she said, "Until the guy's caught, Pete's enforcing increased security surrounding Julia."

"The workouts are about an hour, right?" asked Cash.

Closer to two, but Marley nodded.

"I can drive you," Cash offered, glancing at Marley. "That will give us more flexibility than if you go with the Dardens' driver. As soon as you're done, we can head to the studio."

Her eyes narrowed. There. Once more, she was sure he was hiding something. The easy way he offered such seamless solutions was simply too... smooth. As if he'd already thought through all the possible contingencies. But then, maybe her own past was making her paranoid. That, or the two kisses still burning on her lips. She tried to shake off the feeling. "That won't interfere with your work?"

"I'm the boss," he said easily. "Besides, I work mostly late at night, after the show will be over."

"Okay," Edie finally said while Marley was still considering. Reaching behind her, she rested a hand on the doorknob a moment, then opened the door. Just before she stepped across the threshold, she turned toward Cash. Raising her hand again, as if to brook any argument, she said, "Maybe it's a moot point, but we were going to wind up not seeing each other, anyway. I just want you to know that, Cash."

"I figured," said Cash.

Marley tried not to notice, but she felt a lead weight lifting from her. Maybe what happened in the first moment she'd met Cash was kismet. Their first glance had been electric, and even though he didn't know it, that day had marked an exact year since her divorce. Maybe the distrust she'd felt was unwarranted, just residue left by Chris's betrayal. She had to start trusting her instincts again, didn't she? And yet her gut kept screaming that something about Cash wasn't on the level.

She'd make a few phone calls, she decided. Just to make sure Cash really owned a bar in New Orleans. She wouldn't mind spending some time at his work site, either, to meet the old friend he said he worked for. Maybe her motives weren't pure, but she was sincerely interested in Cash, despite her New Year's resolution. She had to protect herself, though, both her business and her heart.

Edie and Cash were still looking at each other. "You have a nice night," Edie said, sounding gracious for the first time.

Cash nodded. "Thanks, Edie."

And then Edie shut the door, leaving Marley alone with Cash again. As he came toward her, Marley's throat suddenly felt raw, and she licked at lips that had turned dry. "Are you really sure this won't interfere with your schedule?" she managed to say as he stopped in front of her. "Even if you're the boss, aren't you accountable to the friend you're working with?"

"He's understanding," Cash murmured, lifting a

finger and pushing away a lock of hair near her temple. "Especially when something important comes up."

"Important?" she found herself whispering, the voice sounding very far away and completely unlike her own.

"Yeah. Important," he whispered back. "Like this." And then his mouth descended, his lips feathering over hers.

4

"I CAN'T WAIT UNTIL CASH SEES YOU tonight," said a woman named Miranda the next afternoon. The professional makeover artist was dressed in black, from head to toe, and after studying the rack of gowns and accessories in front of her, she poked a long black fingernail into a pile of equally black hair, and said, "You're going to look great."

Maybe. But somehow, the idea of being dressed for national television by a woman who looked like Morticia Adams wasn't very comforting. "I'm more the sweatpants type," Marley offered, eyeing the fancy gowns.

"Tonight's the dinner date," returned Miranda. "Other than the movie premiere, this is your only dress-date. You'll have a chance to look sporty tomorrow, during indoor golfing."

"More my speed."

Nevertheless, after last night's kisses, Marley was feeling a surge of female excitement at the prospect of tantalizing Cash. Besides, she and her ex had met in a rowing club and bonded over athletic interests, while Cash…well, Cash made her feel delicate and hopelessly pretty. She had to admit it was a new—and not entirely unpleasant—sensation. At the door last night, his lips had been almost dry at first, and they'd clung on to hers, blistering with heat, then he'd licked her lips, parting them, and probed with his tongue as his arms slid around her waist, drawing her against him.

Oh, she never wanted to get hurt again. She feared love…or not so much love, but the loss it always seemed to bring. By not loving, she'd hoped to protect herself, but as he'd kissed her, those best-laid plans suddenly seemed so foolish. Maybe she was too young to declare herself permanently single, after all.

She craved touch. All people did. And she shuddered now, remembering his strong body pressed against hers. He'd arched his back, his pelvis hard against hers as his flattened palms moved over her hips, energy radiating from his skin. Quivering, he'd rustled fingers under her shirt and settled his hands just above the waistband of her sweats, on her bare tummy.

He hadn't really groaned, not out loud, but when she'd heard the needy male sigh he'd released, she'd almost asked him to spend the night. Why she'd refrained, she didn't know. The kiss was long and deep, and by the time he'd left, she was drenched with want.

"I'll pick you up tomorrow morning," he'd whispered. "And take you to the Dardens."

She'd barely been able to speak. She hadn't yet fully processed the crazy day. From the moment she'd reached the studio, her whole life had been whisked from her own hands. Her throat, raw by then, had sounded raspy and foreign. "Tomorrow," she'd agreed.

After he'd gone, she'd opened the futon and stretched out, remembering the touch of his hands and how they might have felt, dropping lower, beneath the waistband of her pants. She'd imagined his dark fingers shaking with anticipation as they skated downward, seeking. How, in one day, had she gone from being completely attached to the notion of being single forever, to having her curiosity piqued in a way that couldn't be denied?

"Tomorrow," he'd repeated.

He'd been right on time, too. As she'd gone through the morning routine with Julia, he'd waited discreetly in an enclosed sunroom attached to Sparky Darden's gym. Thankfully, Julia didn't mind the company, and when Sparky Darden stopped by, he'd welcomed Cash. In turn, Cash had done a credible job of explaining why he was accompanying his supposed girlfriend's sister to work, saying he'd brought Marley as a favor to Edie.

Now Marley frowned. Had he lied too easily? Later, she told herself, she would make some calls and insist on visiting the club where he'd been working, to put her mind at ease. She sucked in a breath, barely able to believe any of this was real. Was she in the television studio again, drawn into this strange fantasy life that was to be hers for five days?

She supposed so, because the heavyset, bearded videographer poked his head into the room. "Ready for pictures?"

Miranda nodded. "You can tape until she gets undressed."

Indeed, thought Marley dryly, wondering how models ever got used to this privacy deprivation. Delivery personnel had been arriving in a steady stream, showing Miranda and Marley everything from handbags to clothes to jewelry. She supposed Cash was going through the same thing.

"Don't hide your excitement," the videographer coached as he rolled the tape. "Let the audience see it. We love to play parts of these tapes during the show. People watch the makeover...then see your date wowed by the final product."

"I don't think of myself as a product," Marley said.

"Of course you don't," said Miranda, smiling into the camera as she held up a blue dress. "I think we'll go with this one for the dinner-date segment."

Marley's eyes widened. "It's see-through."

"Now, now," chided Miranda. "It's got a built-in bra and panties. And the color matches your eyes. We call it sea fog." As she held the dress in front of Marley's navy nylon workout suit, Marley forgot the camera was taping. Sure, Cash had said he likes to see a girl in sweatpants, but while she'd been wearing Edie's suit, she'd noticed him staring at her legs and trying to glimpse inside the jacket, seemingly hungry for silk and lace. But this...

Would make Cash Champagne crazy with lust. The transparent blue three-quarter-length sleeves were tattered looking, as was the hem, almost as if some man had already tried to rip the gown from a body. The weave of the fabric became more dense in key areas, at the neck and shoulders, over her breasts and around her hips. Otherwise, the dress was as deceptively insubstantial as a spider's web. "It's cold out for it."

"We've got a matching blue velvet cape," assured Miranda. She waved Vinny through the door, saying, "Get lost. Marley needs to put this on now."

As the man vanished, Marley couldn't help but smile. She felt like Cinderella. It really was a role reversal, since Edie was the romantic. But just for one night...

"You've got the perfect figure for it. Here. Turn around and let me zip this up. You must take working out seriously."

I used to. She still ran at least six miles, lifted weights and spent time on the machines, but whenever she contemplated the junk food she'd eaten on the sly since her divorce, she could kick herself. "I'm a—" Remembering she was supposed to be Edie, she corrected herself. "My *sister's* a fitness trainer," she continued. "She's taught me a lot."

Fortunately, Miranda's mind had moved on to other matters. "You'll be wearing diamonds on loan from Cartier, and I've got the perfect box-shaped bag that hangs from a rope. Once we pile your hair on top of your head, you'll look as if you just stepped out of another century."

Marley definitely felt as if she were living someone else's life. Behind the scenes, the television studio was wild—full of people all seemingly type A personalities rushing every which way. Marley wasn't a big fan of the tube, largely because she liked to spend her free time outside, enjoying nature, but she had a renewed appreciation for the hard work that went into the shows.

Sighing with satisfaction, Miranda turned Marley toward the mirror. "What do you think?

Marley barely recognized herself. "I'm not sure what I think," she murmured, "but Cash is going to be blown away."

"WHAT A NIGHT," Cash murmured as the last dish was cleared away, his voice made huskier by the wine they'd been drinking. He nuzzled Marley's neck, then glanced around Alexandria's again, suddenly remembering to flash a smile toward Vinny the videographer and the NBC cameras that were trained on them. Pricy and cozy, this Italian eatery on the Upper West Side was dazzling, like eye candy. Tilting back a goblet of burgundy, Cash let it glide down his throat. It went effortlessly, a slow burn of heat spiraling to his gut. "This is the best wine I've ever had."

She arched a brow. "Ah. You're an expert on wine, too?"

"I own a bar."

"You weren't drinking that night in the comedy club."

She said it almost as if she'd caught him in a lie, and while he didn't want to comment on her obvious distrust, it leaked sideways into all their conversations, and it was starting to grate. He shrugged. "I got my start as a bartender, and in that position, you wind up seeing a lot of sloppy drunks. I try to make sure I never look like them."

"So, you do drink?"

"Whiskey, usually." At least when he drank. He swirled the wine in the glass again and lifted it toward her, barely aware the cameras were trained on them, since she'd captured his whole attention. "Wine, on occasion, when it's good." He took another sip. The bouquet was complex, the wine full-bodied and well-aged, and the taste burst in his mouth like the kiss he'd shared with Marley last night. "And this is good," he added.

She nestled so they were shoulder-to-shoulder, both with their elbows on the table. "You like this place?"

"Yeah." He liked being on a date with her. The dress. Everything. Even the cameras. Leaning closer, he nodded toward them, using his eyes to tell her to smile, and she chuckled softly.

"Really, it's not that bad," she murmured.

"What?"

"What we've gotten ourselves involved in."

He couldn't help but chuckle. "You like the cameras?"

She made a point of fluttering her eyes for them. "It's safe," she teased. "There's only so much you'll do to me if all America is watching."

He smiled back. "Don't be too sure."

Pursing her lips in a scarcely suppressed smile, she glanced toward the cameras again, then took in the restaurant. The place was magical. Cash had been in restaurant-related businesses for years—this kind of work was in his blood—but he'd never seen anything like this. Trees grew inside, and the branches that stretched to the ceiling, as well as the trunks, were covered with tiny white lights. Huge suspended bubbles, the amber color of champagne, floated above them, drifting through the branches, apparently propelled by jets of air that came from artfully placed vents; they were engineered so that the bubbles never dropped below ten or so feet, and patrons could stroll beneath them. Oversize white-lace tablecloths covered round tables, draping to a white-carpeted floor, so it was hard to tell where the table linen ended and the floor began. Elaborate sterling candelabra were everywhere, and tall white tapers burned, instead of electric lighting.

Marley looked a little nervous. "Not my usual style."

"Mine, neither," he agreed, his eyes roving over her, "but I can't say I mind." Even his suit was surprisingly comfortable, practical and black, loose in the shoulders, with wide jacket lapels and roomy trousers. Cash could have done without the silver silk tie, but as far as ties went, this one was made to be tied loosely, so he didn't feel like he was choking. "And I hate ties."

"You look good in one, though."

The comment gave him more pleasure than it should have. "Thanks, but nothing could do you justice."

She smiled. "Thanks." She paused. "What's your bar like?"

"In New Orleans?" He shrugged. "A juke joint. But it's on Bourbon Street. I get a lot of tourists, and I know a booking agent who's landed some great blues bands." He watched her eyes widen as he named a few.

"Impressive."

"It's been good. I like the pace of it. The hours. I've got a manager I trust, too, a woman named Annie Dean, so I can spend time fishing."

"What?" she teased. "You sound retired at thirty."

"Thirty-five," he corrected. "And I'm considering my next move. I'm a coinvestor with a friend here, but we're talking about starting other ventures together." Hardly interested in talking about work, he reached to touch the fabric of her dress. The sleeve was as light as air.

But she wasn't about to be sidetracked. "And Cash Champagne," she said. "Is that a real name?"

His eyes widened. "Uh...yeah. Why?"

He could see the embarrassed color rising on her cheeks, even though the lights were dim. "Sorry, but it sounds kind of...made up."

He considered and guessed she had a point. "Only if you live in the northeast," he countered, "where everyone's named things such as Karen Smith."

"Not me," she returned.

He shrugged. "My mother married a French guy from the bayou, which is where I got Champagne. And she loved listening to Johnny Cash." She stared at him a moment, and he could tell the exact moment she decided that his explanation made sense. "Are you always so distrustful?"

"Only since the divorce." As if wanting to change the subject, she glanced toward the cameras again, suddenly flashing a smile for their benefit, but saying, "This is exciting, but I do feel a little nervous about being watched."

"By me or the crowd?"

She answered with a smile, her lips looking kissable, darkened by the wine that was flowing through his blood. "Both."

"Forget about the cameras. Just look at me." A film crew surrounded them, and people had stopped to stare inside the restaurant's windows, probably hoping big-name stars were being filmed.

Marley's chuckle was as effervescent as the bubbles circulating above them, and he had to admit that, as much as he liked seeing her in sports clothes, the dress was heart-stopping.

"C'mon," she murmured. "It's hard to eat with a bunch of people watching you."

"True. I've never felt that self-conscious about my table manners in my life." He shrugged. "I'm used to crawdads served on newspaper, and I can't say I've had pumpkin-stuffed ravioli."

"Served with cinnamon sauce."

He snuggled closer, unsure which he was playing to more—her or the studio audience that would see snippets of tape from their night together. "It was good." He ducked to kiss her, not firm, hard and deep, as he'd done at the door last night, but just a nip, a promise.

"This dress is amazing," he drawled, not for the first time, the wine dripping in his voice, slowing his words to muted cadences. Her hair was styled the way he liked it, unlike her sister's, so that tendrils framed her face, just touching cheekbones that a makeup artist had glossed with glittering powder.

In fact, every inch of her shimmered like a river at night, and the scent she wore was strange, exotic and peppery; the spicy edge of it hit him like an aphrodisiac. Whenever he took a breath, it tunneled to his lungs and heat gathered in his belly. No woman had ever made him feel this way, not that he'd tell her. Still, this substantiated the theory of his buddy, Sam Beaujolais, that on a relational level, everything boiled down to sex. According to Sam, if things were right in bed, everything else had a way of working itself out.

Maybe. But Cash figured he and Marley were an exception. Oh, his blood was dancing, all right. Everything was sharper. Brighter. More in focus. The starkly cold night felt delicious. The stars seemed to burst in the black sky. But she'd find out what he really wanted, eventually. That meant it was unfair to notice how she seemed to perk up for the cameras. Was she simply playing for them? Trying to win? When he'd caught himself wondering, he'd admitted he'd rather be alone with her, because then he'd know her gestures—the fluttering lashes and husky voice and sudden dart of her tongue—were for him. Only him.

"Care to share any of those deep thoughts?"

He shook his head. "Not really."

She considered, then said, "I hope Julia's all right."

He didn't want to sound too curious. "Me, too."

Marley took a sip, and he watched her throat work as she swallowed, how the soft shake of her head made the diamonds hanging from her ears glint in the light of burning tapers. Pale pinks and baby blues shattered in refracting light against her glittery cheeks. The diamond at her neck hung on a smoky blue velvet choker, and while it was just as arresting, it paled by comparison to her eyes. Dark and smoky, they looked like two ancient gems.

His gaze skated over her. Beneath the see-through material, he could make out the swell of her breasts. With her no longer wearing a restraining sports bra, he could see her breasts were fuller than he'd imagined, and as the material shifted, it dropped dangerously low, almost exposing nipples that beaded under the flimsy fabric. Realizing his mouth had gone dry, he glanced away, only to find himself staring at the cameras again.

"Edie said Julia's been getting threats," he managed to say, trying to appear natural and looking away, taking another sip of wine, hoping it might take the edge off how her near proximity was affecting him.

"Letters," Marley clarified. "Someone started sending them after her wedding was announced. Pete Shriver—he's that guy you saw today at the Darden estate near the guard booth by the front gate— he's head of security. He's trying to catch them."

"Any leads?" Cash couldn't help but ask.

As she shook her head, the long diamond earrings jangled again. Before he thought it through, Cash had ducked his head, caught one between his teeth and nibbled her lobe.

She sucked in a breath. "I bet the cameras liked that," she said, sounding breathless.

"It wasn't for the cameras, Marley," he whispered, flicking his tongue in her ear and blowing softly.

"Shouldn't you be calling me Edie?"

"Probably. But I'd rather call you Marley." His lips were close enough to her ear that the cameras wouldn't pick up on their movement. No one in the viewing audience could read his lips.

She blew out a shaky breath, and returned to the initial conversation. "I think Pete located the mailbox from which the guy's mailing the letters."

"How did he do that?"

"I don't know. He's a trained security person. I guess they have their ways. I think Edie said the mailbox is on Ninety-Sixth Street." He watched her frown, how her barely visible blond eyebrows knitted. They'd been plucked to faint arches he had an urge to trace with his tongue. "I just hope nothing happens," she continued. "It would be tragic. Julia's so in love."

"So, they really think she's in danger?"

"Pete believes the perpetrator is an enemy of Mr. Darden's. He's made a lot over the years."

Cash was very careful not to say anything.

Marley continued. "I'm worried about something ruining the wedding, too, for Edie's sake. She's afraid Julia and Lorenzo will get fed up and elope."

"Why don't they?"

"Mr. Darden insisted on a wedding. He dotes on Julia."

"His only child," Cash murmured.

Like many people in America, Cash knew the story. Sparky had married only once, a Hollywood starlet who'd made a couple pictures. She'd given up her career, given birth to Julia, and then died just two years after the marriage.

Not taking his eyes from Marley, Cash murmured, "What made Julia's mother different?"

"Different?"

He nodded. "From the other starlets?"

Marley shook her head. "What makes love happen for anyone?"

"Public rumor had it that Sparky Darden's a womanizer."

As if wanting to lighten the mood, she said, "In my case, I claim youth, hormones and stupidity."

"You're only a year older now than when you divorced."

"In years only. At heart, I'm now a stone cynic."

"I don't believe it."

She stared at him a long moment, then suddenly laughed. "As far as my distrust of you is concerned," she said, "I don't have to worry. No doubt, Pete Shriver's checking you out." Her teasing smile widened. "Ah. Now you look worried. Do you have something to hide?"

"Would I tell you if I did?"

"Interesting answer."

"Maybe we need more interesting questions."

"Got any ideas?"

"Plenty. I'd love to elude these cameramen."

"Last night we got lucky, but now they know we've got a yen to escape, so I don't think we're going to get away."

He glanced toward the cameras once more, then his eyes found hers. "Do you want to?"

"Yes and no."

It wasn't the answer he'd been hoping for. Not that he welcomed the emotions she solicited. They were too strong, the kind that could threaten to get of control. The last thing Cash wanted was to feel passions rule him again. Not love, nor lust and least of all, revenge.

Bringing her hand upward, he brushed his lips across her skin, his eyes never leaving hers, then he snaked his other hand around the column of her neck, stroking skin that was even softer than the velvet choker.

Purring, she released a shivery sound that shot through his system, making him feel he had no choice but to urge her mouth to his. At the liquid touch, fiery heat and salt mixed with the thick bouquet of the wine. "You taste good," he whispered thickly, "but I want more." He buried his face in her neck, so the cameras couldn't read his lips. "You in bed." He had no right, but he had to ask. "Are you just playing for the cameras, or do you want this as much as I do?"

He leaned back a fraction, hungry for the answer, his eyes pulling over the gown, settling once more on her unrestrained breasts that begged for his touch. "Marley," he whispered hoarsely. "Say something. Answer me." Burning need infused every inch of him. Between his legs, he suddenly ached.

"I…"

"…Know you don't trust men, Marley, but that's not what I'm asking."

"On a purely physical level—" Her voice caught. "My feelings mirror yours."

His eyes seared, flicking over her breasts and the ready buds he couldn't touch because they were surrounded by the cameras. Watching the tips of her breasts bead beneath the dress was like torture. Yes…the dress was so delicate, it would disintegrate beneath his tongue, he imagined. He actually ducked, ready to lick it from her body, his throat raw with what he was about to do….

And then, once more, he remembered they were being taped.

5

"DADDY?" JULIA GLANCED at the TV. "Are you sure you're okay? You didn't listen to a word Lozo and I said at dinner."

"I'm a bit tired," Sparky admitted.

"I'm so sorry, Daddy!"

Clutching the remote, Sparky patted a spot beside him on the bed. Keeping his eyes on *Rate the Dates*, he put his arm around his daughter, urging her to snuggle. "Did Lorenzo go home?"

"No," she said, resting her head on his shoulder. "He's staying overnight."

Sparky's lips pursed, but he didn't say anything. Supposedly, when he didn't have early morning practice sessions, Lorenzo slept in a guest bedroom to avoid the long drive back to his Manhattan apartment, but Sparky knew his soon-to-be son-in-law sneaked into Julia's room. After all, Sparky wasn't born yesterday, and he did have his own security staff.

"Can I get you something, Daddy? Hot cocoa. Or tea?"

Whiskey would be better, but Sparky's doctor had forbidden it, so the only bottle in the house was the one he kept hidden in his study. "Not a thing," he said distractedly as he studied the couple having dinner in Alexandria's, surrounded by floating champagne bubbles. Very romantic. Both contestants were dressed to kill. Her, in a see-through blue dress that was making every man in America drool. Him, in a dark designer suit that was probably doing the same for female viewers.

They looked as smitten as Sparky's daughter was with her hockey player. He just hoped they won. Although they were unaware of it, he had an interest in the Benning sisters, and it was no accident he'd chosen Edie to plan Julia's wedding. While the sisters knew nothing about Sparky's connection to their family, someone close to them did, but that person had decided to remain silent....

On-screen, the couple looked positively dreamy-eyed, their lips dark red from the wine, and it was already clear they were going to win. Not only had they been chosen as the underdog couple, which always gave contestants an edge, but every second, they acted as if they were going to kiss. Judging from the smoldering glances, they wouldn't stop at a smooch, either.

Sparky half hoped they'd run off again tonight, the way they had last night. Tonight's segment began with Trevor Milane showing a tape from *Rate the Dates* security videos, depicting the couple eluding a videographer and vanishing into the night. It was the first time a couple had hidden from the cameras in the history of the show.

The two other couples were boring by comparison, he thought as they cut to commercial break. One was from New Jersey, and they had big hairdos and accents that grated on Sparky's every last nerve. The other couple—two tall, blond tennis players with tight smiles and out-of-season suntans—was from Connecticut and just as predictable.

Neither couple was putting on a show as juicy as Cash and Edie! Or was it a show? Maybe they were really falling in love in front of the cameras. Sparky waited patiently, then he peered at the screen as the commercial break ended and Trevor Milane said, "We're back. We've watched how all our contestants have handled a dinner date, and while we won't tally scores until the end, each of you should think about which date should win!"

Sparky considered Cash Champagne. He seemed to be a good choice for Edie, and it was nice of him to bring her sister Marley to the estate in the mornings. Thinking of the differences between the sisters, Sparky couldn't help but smile. Marley was tougher and athletic, with wild, spiraling golden blond curls, and a body that wouldn't quit. By contrast, Edie was softer in every way, more conventionally feminine and graceful, and probably harder to get to know. A young man like Cash would have to slowly peel back the layers over her truest nature....

On-screen, Cash looked up to the task—listening attentively, leaning ever closer, his eyes riveted to his date's. During Julia's workout, Sparky had spoken to him for some time. He was hard to read, with eyes that didn't give much away, and he was a New Orleans boy, too, which Sparky appreciated. Originally from North Carolina, Sparky loved the South. That part of the country had been good to him, and until his illness, he'd spent most of his time there, only using this house when he visited New York, which was where he'd first started his hotel business.

Yes, Cash was just the kind of man Sparky liked, and he'd been pleased to find that the bartender was helping a friend open a club uptown. Because most hotels had bars, Sparky knew that business well, and he'd enjoyed the shoptalk.

"Lozo and I are bored," Julia wheedled now. "Pete won't even let us go to a movie. He's sticking to us like glue, and while I know you love me, Daddy..."

"I'm worried," Sparky countered as she toyed with the few silver strands of hair he had left. For weeks, Julia had been begging him to call Pete Shriver off her tail. "Until the person who's sending the letters is caught, this is how things have to be."

"But not around the house, Daddy," she protested.

Maybe she had a point. According to Pete, the threats were probably meant to be a scare tactic, and over the past few months, absolutely no attempt had been made to harm Julia, or Sparky.

"Pete's following us everywhere," she said again.

Sparky felt himself weakening. While he knew he shouldn't give his baby girl so much power over him, he loved her, and the thought of her discomfort pained him, especially since no one had made any real attempt to hurt her.

"Daddy," she began again. "Pete doesn't even want me going into the city to get my hair done. And Marley and I have to work out here, instead of at the gym in town. We can't go to Big Apple Brides for planning meetings." She grunted in frustration. "Please tell him to back off."

"Okay," Sparky conceded. "Just around the house, though. And I want you staying on the estate."

As Cash Champagne rose, Sparky's attention returned to the TV. He watched as Cash leaned, grasping Edie's hand and pulling her to her feet, then he frowned.

Something teased his consciousness, something faint and ephemeral that he couldn't quite capture. But what? And then it hit him. Just for a second, Sparky could swear he'd seen Cash Champagne before, and not during Marley and Julia's workouts. But where?

"ARE YOU ALONE, MARLEY?" Viv Benning asked after Marley had answered the phone, her excited curiosity giving away the hope that her daughter was occupied with male company.

"Afraid so. Have you forgotten your daughters are cursed when it comes to romance?"

"You're not!" exclaimed Viv. As if to prove it, she continued. "Not only are you dating again, but Cash is gorgeous. Your Granny Ginny just made up that story about the curse, so you girls would work harder at finding someone."

"And that was necessary...?"

"Because she's a paranoid older woman who was born at a time when women *had* to get married, since the only job available was being somebody's wife."

"So, you think Granny Ginny's using scare tactics to encourage us to finds mates, huh?"

"Absolutely. There is no curse, Marley."

Marley thought of the three men Edie dated one year, all of whom ditched her and married somebody else, but she decided not to reiterate the history of failed Benning romances right now. It would only depress her mother. "When's Granny visiting, anyway?"

"Friday. And you're expected to be here."

"That's the last night of the show," Marley murmured.

"You say that as if seeing your grandmother could actually jinx the outcome," Viv chided.

Marley refrained from saying that was exactly what she'd been thinking. It didn't portend well that she'd gotten railroaded onto a prime-time dating show the very same week her grandmother was visiting. Although Granny was the mother of Viv's first husband, a man from Florida named Jasper Hartley whom the girls couldn't remember since they'd been so young when he'd died, Joe Benning, the only father the girls had known, had always welcomed Granny Ginny into their home.

Keeping tabs on her granddaughters was one of Granny's greatest pleasures in life, and with her only son deceased, the Bennings were the only family Granny really had left. Shortly after her husband had died, a then twenty-four-year-old Viv had returned from Florida to New York, where her own mother had offered to help raise the babies. Joe was the carpenter hired to turn a small Village apartment into a space better equipped for kids, and the rest was history....

Now Marley wondered if she should bring Cash to meet Granny, and a smile curled her lips. He'd probably be shocked to hear more about the curse from Granny Ginny. No doubt, he'd turn tail and run, finding out what he was up against. And shouldn't Marley be glad about that, since she didn't trust him?

Be that as it may, she just wished she hadn't wound up alone tonight. All evening, she'd fantasized Cash would take her home, remove the blue dress and make love to her. In reality, they'd been rushed to the studio as soon as the cameras stopped rolling at Alexandria's, hustled into separate dressing rooms, then stripped by the staff. Apparently, Cartier was very anxious to ensure the return of their diamonds, and Gucci wanted his dress and suit back.

It had been…a letdown. Which was good, Marley told herself firmly. By the time Cash had brought her home, the January night had hit her like the proverbial cold shower, and she'd remembered that, despite the attraction, she had a very bad gut feeling about him. She'd kissed him, but without the heat they'd generated on-screen. Earlier, because America had been watching, exploring the attraction was safer, since nothing more than a kiss was allowed. Once they were alone, however…

Well, she'd wanted him to leave. But now, paradoxically, she was sorry he was gone. Marley's mother had been waiting dutifully to hear more juicy details, and when they weren't forthcoming, she said, "Did you get the tape, Marley?"

Yawning, Marley stared down at the remote in her hand, then hit Play. "I was just starting to watch it. Thanks for leaving it in my mailbox. This looks like the first show." She froze the frame, so they could talk. She'd gotten to the point in the broadcast where she was telling Trevor Milane she didn't want to do the show. Swallowing hard, she wondered how she'd react to seeing the next episode. She really had felt like Cinderella tonight, dressing in fine clothes and diamonds….

As soon as Viv had realized her daughter was on the air, she'd started taping. "Pop and I were watching the show, anyway, the first night," she said now. "As I saw you, I started recording. I couldn't believe it was really you. My own little baby on TV. It came right out of the blue. I taped tonight's show, too. You have to see how great you look. Like a movie star."

Marley winced. "You're such a mother."

"No," Viv protested. "Really! I could almost see you going into acting. And Cash is so cute. I'm glad Edie wound up going along with this. She said there were no sparks between her and Cash, but you two seem to be hitting it off. I can't wait to watch you on the movie premiere date. Maybe you'll meet some movie people." Pausing to swoon, her mother added, "Like Sean Connery."

Marley sighed. "Maybe I should bring Cash to meet Granny on Friday." As she said it, she wasn't sure about the idea, even if he'd agree, which she doubted. He'd dated Edie, if only casually, so it seemed a bit weird. Besides, he'd avoided the family previously, and Edie had said she'd felt it was intentional, something else that had made Marley distrust him. "This week, I can't come for dinner because of the show," continued Marley. "At noon, they start taping the dates." That, too, was a little strange. Activities were arranged back-to-back, so Marley felt as if she were going to a well-organized summer camp, rather than being filmed for TV.

"I know. And don't worry," her mom added. "We're not telling anyone you two switched." She giggled. "I used to love it when you'd fool us. It's been years…"

Marley wasn't in the mood to rehash the countless family stories involving the theme of playing switcheroo, but her heart suddenly swelled, and she wondered when she and Edie had drifted apart. They'd been so inseparable as kids, and they were still close, but it had been hard to be twins, and in their drive to forge individual identities, she sometimes thought they'd gone too far. Her voice softened. "We did have fun."

"You still do. You're just going through a phase. Now, I've got to run. Since you can't make dinner, call when you decide which day for breakfast."

"I've got to give Julia her workouts, Mom."

"Take a day off," Viv suggested pragmatically. Right before she hung up, she added, "And bring Cash. Your father and I need to meet the man who's on TV with our baby girl."

Sighing once more, Marley hit Play again. She was relieved to find she looked better on TV than she would have imagined. The suit was becoming, even though it was more Edie's style, and the makeup artists were right. On screen, the garish makeup wasn't nearly as overpowering as Marley had feared.

"Strange," she whispered as she watched Cash rise, turn away from the camera and hunker down, placing his hands on either armrest of her chair. She very distinctly remembered shrinking backward, feeling trapped. Now her lips parted in surprise as she watched herself scoot forward, wreathe her arms around his neck and pull him toward her with wanton abandon. It was one of the hottest kisses she'd ever witnessed.

As soon as the kiss ended, Marley shifted her attention to the phone, which was still in her hand. There was no doubt now. She had to find out more about Cash. Already, she'd phoned him at the club uptown, and had been surprised to find he was exactly where he'd said he'd be.

"Why, you sneaky girl," he'd drawled. "Checking up on me?"

He'd been joking, but she'd flushed with guilt. "Of course not!" she'd protested.

Now she glanced at the clock. It was 11:00 p.m., which meant the bar he'd said he owned in New Orleans would be open. What had Edie said the name of the place was? *The Cash Cow.* "That's right," she murmured. Calling New Orleans information, she said, "Could I have a number for the Cash Cow, please? It's a club on Bourbon Street."

As the automated voice gave the number, she jotted it on one of the coffee-ringed magazines strewn across the coffee table. Then she hung up and dialed, trying to remember the name of the manager, and wondering how to ask questions discreetly, and if she should use her own name. The phone clicked on, and a female voice with an accent so thick Marley barely understood her, drawled, "Cash Cow."

Marley considered hanging up. There was still time. Instead, she said, "May I speak to Annie Dean?"

"MY MUSCLES ARE BURNING," Julia complained good-naturedly the next morning as she and Marley ran along a wooded snow-covered path on the estate's property, their cleated shoes leaving tracks behind them in white powder.

Marley punched the air, keeping her arms moving. "We could have stayed inside." Julia still needed to exercise on the machines and finish the weight-lifting routine Marley had devised specifically for her.

Flipping up the hood of Lorenzo's running jacket, Julia grinned, clearly not really minding the harsh weather. "I'm game for another mile. Lozo loves these legs muscles I'm getting."

"Good." Marley grinned back. As she'd told Cash this morning in the truck, it was hard to believe Julia was an heiress, since she was as unpretentious as any girl next door. Cash had only pulled the truck over to the curb, hauled her beneath him in the seat, and delivered a series of sloppy, open-mouthed kisses, as if to say he had much better things to do than discuss Julia Darden. Laughing, Marley had squirmed, kissing him back even as she fought him. She'd gotten him in a headlock. "Can't you even carry on a normal conversation, Cash?"

He'd tried to shake her off. "Not with you around."

"I'm that tempting?"

"Yeah. Every time we get away from the cameras."

Once they were on the road again, she'd tamped down her guilt about calling his club the previous night. Still, she'd learned he really did own it, and while the manager, Annie Dean, hadn't been available, the person who'd answered had taken a message. The manager had never called back, but the exchange had helped put Marley's mind at ease.

"Running in the woods is a real treat," she said

now. In the city, the trail around the Central Park Reservoir was wooded, but Marley avoided it for safety reasons, and while the West Side Highway was safer, the running path was of concrete. Here, through the trees and over a hill to her right, she glimpsed a rural highway, but otherwise, she could imagine she was miles from civilization. She glanced behind them. "Did we lose Pete?"

"Yep," Julia said with a grin. "I had another talk with Daddy about surveillance. I love Pete, but he goes overboard, trying to please Daddy. The threats have been coming for months, nothing's happened, and most likely I'd be attacked in the city, anyway, where its easy for crazy lunatics to hide in a crowd. Somebody's just trying to shake me up and ruin my wedding, and I'm not going to let them."

Marley shot Julia an appreciative glance. While she admired Julia's ability to stay calm under pressure, Pete's tail had made Marley feel safer. Even if no attempt had been made on Julia, she was still getting all those creepy letters.

Oblivious of her thoughts and sounding faintly winded, Julia said, "How long's Cash been dating Edie?"

Marley blinked, regrouping. It was hard to remember she was playing the third wheel, the unattached, divorced sister, unlucky in love. "Uh…about a month."

"It's nice of him to drive you. Daddy could have sent a car." Julia grinned. "Cash must be trying to impress Edie by getting to know you. I love it when guys do things like that for family. Lozo's always taking Daddy to fancy restaurants. He's a meat-and-potatoes man, but he tries everything from snails to arugula just because Daddy likes exotic food." Dodging a limb that had fallen across the snowy path, she continued, "Cash and Edie sizzle. I watched the show with Daddy last night."

Marley's jealousy was senseless, but she didn't want people thinking Edie, not she, was the beneficiary of Cash's attention. The emotion was strong enough to give her pause. No…she couldn't deny it. She was becoming quickly attached to Cash—as it turned out, he was fun to be around—and at least this week, there was no way to escape him. Vaguely, she wondered if she would if she could.

Suddenly, she tilted her head, slowing her steps. Julia squinted. "What?"

Marley had slowed to a walking jog. "I'm not sure." She scanned the trees, trying to pinpoint what had claimed her attention. "I don't know."

Nothing seemed out of the ordinary in the woods, but Marley's senses had gone on alert. Everything seemed too quiet. She felt overly conscious of the cold seeping through her running suit, and startled when leaves rustled in the evergreens. Wings flapped…a flock of birds took flight. Her eyes followed them—the span of opening wings, the arrowlike precision as the birds moved into formation. She didn't want to alarm Julia, but…

"Pete!" Marley yelled just as she saw what had alarmed her—fresh footprints in the snow, about fifteen feet ahead. She heard a crack. Maybe Pete was behind them, closer than they'd assumed. "Get down," she whispered, hunkering and glancing around, wondering which way they should run. "Get down," she said again, but Julia didn't move. Had a gun sounded?

"I think a car backfired," said Julia. "On the highway."

"Maybe, but go back, anyway, Julia."

"Not if you don't—"

Another crack sounded. Wood splintered nearby, and when Marley's eyes followed the sound, she saw the tree the bullet had hit. At least that's what she assumed had happened. Bark had ripped away, exposing new yellow wood. She took off running, sensing rather than seeing Julia fall back.

"Who's out here!" she yelled on impulse, her eyes panning the trees as she neared the footprints. What was she doing? she suddenly thought. She'd acted on instinct, but she was running toward the sound, not away from it, and the guy had a gun. Her heart stuttered.

Rustling sounded. It was close. Then rapid footsteps crunched on frozen leaves. They were pounding now. Closer. Ahead, to the right, a dark figure suddenly crashed through the brush, visible only a fraction of a second before darting into a cover of trees. He was moving faster now, and he was carrying a rifle.

He plummeted over the hill toward the highway. Pivoting, Marley plunged over the hill, also. He was running hard, so she'd hear him if he stopped, she reasoned, and with trees between them, she had cover. He must have parked on the highway. Maybe she could get a license number. Maybe on the basis of that, Pete could catch this guy and end the whole ordeal. Edie would be so relieved, once the threat hanging over Julia was removed. The burning heat of winter wind tortured Marley's lungs as she careened downward, her shoes sliding on frozen ground. She was fast—probably faster than him, but he had a head start.

Suddenly, she felt disoriented. She almost stopped. She was surrounded by trees now, in a thicket. How had she lost track of him? She must have. Steps were coming from the opposite direction now. Had she gotten turned around in the woods? Been confused by all this white snow? Or was someone else on the path? An accomplice? In the periphery of her vision, a dark figure suddenly lunged between trees. Was it the same man? Someone different? She had no time to find out. He was flying at her.

And then he hit her, full force. The impact took her breath, and she went down hard, snow breaking the fall. How had he been so quiet? Why hadn't she heard him? Clawing at him, keeping her head down, she went for his face. Skin peeled under her nails. She felt the warmth of blood. He gasped as she jabbed at his throat, drew back her knee and kicked, but she got his thigh, not his groin.

He grunted in pain. "Marley. Dammit."

Just as she registered that her attacker was Cash, the heavy body imprisoning her was gone. He rolled off, leaped to his feet and took off running again, disappearing over the hill, running for the highway, the tails of his dark coat blowing. She rolled to her feet, sprinting after him as a car engine roared to life.

The vehicle sounded big. A truck or an SUV. Tires squealed. He was getting away. Where was Pete?

Was Julia safe? She couldn't believe Cash had tackled her. He must have thought she was the shooter. Banking sideways, she used the sides of her sneakers to skid, letting soggy leaves and mud carry her down the embankment. At the bottom, she hurdled a guardrail and ran onto the empty two-lane roadway toward Cash, who was crouched down, looking at the tire tracks. "Did you see anything?" she called.

"Black SUV," he said over his shoulder, rising to his feet. "The plates were covered with mud. You? Did you get a look at him?"

"No. He was dressed in black—" Panting more from fear than exertion, she halted her words, trying to catch her breath. "I think he wore a hat. Maybe even a ski mask. I couldn't tell. He was fast, and I was behind him. He had a rifle. I saw that."

As Cash turned toward her, she realized he was furious. "What were you doing?" he demanded. "Chasing him like that? He had a rifle, Marley. And I thought you were him."

"What was I supposed to do?" she countered. As Cash came toward her, his long jeans-clad legs eating up the pavement, she shrugged, not entirely sure why she hadn't responded more sensibly. "I acted on instinct," she managed to say, piecing together the past few minutes and feeling a rush of pique that he wasn't complimenting her bravery. "Maybe it wasn't smart, Cash, but…"

Reaching her, he wrapped an arm around her and dragged her into his arms. Folding into the embrace and feeling the hard welcoming warmth of his body, she leaned back a fraction, to look into thunderous eyes. "You could have gotten killed," he muttered, brushing his own windblown black locks from his face.

She shrugged. "He was in front of me, running, and he wasn't going to turn around. If he did, I figured I'd hear him. Besides," she pointed out. "*You* were chasing him."

Shiny and intense, his eyes looked particularly dark and bright in the milky morning light. Piercing through the gray like stars in fog, they seemed to say that this was no time for one of Marley's pro-female-power speeches. "I sometimes teach self-defense," she reminded him.

"No kidding," he muttered. "You nearly got me where it counts."

"And I scratched your face," she said, sucking a breath through clenched teeth as she lifted a finger and traced the thin red line on his cheek. "Sorry."

"I'll live."

She mustered a smile. "Otherwise, I'm glad I missed."

"Me, too." He touched her shoulder gently, then the arm she'd wrapped around his waist, as if making sure she was still in one piece. After that, he brushed away a spiraling blond wave that had edged from beneath her hat. "You're okay?"

"I think so. Where's Pete?"

"I hear him up on the path. Apparently Julia's been begging her dad to call off the guards."

Marley pricked up her ears. Far off, she could hear voices approaching, too. "And this happens on the first day Pete actually leaves Julia alone," she muttered. "Good timing."

Cash shook his head. "More likely, the guy's been

watching Julia, and when the security was loosened, he made his move."

Marley inhaled sharply. "Not a comforting thought."

"No," said Cash, ducking his head, so his lips hovered above hers. "It means this isn't just a scare tactic. Somebody's really after her." Leaning another fraction, he briefly claimed her mouth, his lips locking between hers, clinging a moment before letting go.

She tried to ignore how his worry over her safety was affecting her—doing strange things to her pulse and making her want to kiss him again. And again. It was obvious Cash was starting to care, and that thought, more than the danger, solicited a shivery breath.

"You could have been hurt," he repeated.

"Maybe I shouldn't have chased him," she conceded. In fact, the more Marley thought about it, and saw the danger reflected in Cash's eyes, the more she realized she or Julia could have been killed. "I didn't think," she admitted. "I just wanted to catch him. I guess I was thinking mostly of Edie." Julia, too. Both women had drummed it into Marley's head that the letters were only meant to put a wrench in the wedding, as if this were merely a mean-spirited prank. "I wanted to make sure nothing would stop the wedding…."

"The guy had a gun."

She considered a long moment, then said what had been on her mind the last couple of minutes. "Uh…so do you, Cash." She'd seen the weapon in his hand as soon as she'd reached the pavement, and now, before the security staff joined them, she wanted an explanation. She watched Cash pocket the revolver. "Do you always carry that?"

He considered a long moment, his eyes getting that dark, filmy cast, exactly the look that made her distrust him. "Most of the time."

"I'm surprised Pete didn't frisk you."

"Me, too," he said simply. "But I came here with you."

That thought brought absolutely no comfort. Could someone use her or Edie to get close to Julia? Was he? Her nape prickled as she pushed aside the thought. After all, he clearly wasn't the bad guy, since he'd been chasing the man with the rifle. She blew out a shaky breath. Was it really this easy to breach the Darden's supposedly state-of-the-art security, even if Pete had been asked to lay low? Cash had walked in with a gun, and while most of the property was surrounded by high gates or electrified fence, this area skirted a highway; the guy in the SUV had simply parked and walked onto the estate.

She shivered from both the close call and the cold. What if her initial instincts about Cash had been right? What if he'd had some ulterior motive for dating Edie? "Why did you bring a gun here, Cash?" she asked.

He eyed her for a long time, then said the last thing she expected. "I used to be a cop."

6

"CASH WILL BE OUT IN A MINUTE, so relax and get comfortable in the Jacuzzi," a technician said the next afternoon. "Try to pretend we're not here, Edie."

Yeah, right. The blue string-bikini Miranda had chosen for Marley to wear was so insubstantial that it could untie itself and drift away in the hot tub currents with all of America watching. Squinting into lights bright enough to illuminate a football stadium, Marley took a final glance around the Upper East Side spa club where they were taping, taking in the crews setting up cameras all around her, and then she shut her eyes and thought, *A cop.*

She should have guessed. Cash's previous employment explained the wary caution she'd seen in his eyes and the sense of danger she'd felt. It accounted for the animal grace of his body, too, not to mention the license he'd shown her that allowed him to own a gun, albeit, she suspected, not to carry it.

His story checked out. She wasn't proud of it, but she'd called the New Orleans Police Department this morning. Not only was she told Cash had been an officer before leaving to open his club, but the woman to whom she'd spoken had taken Marley's name and number, apologizing profusely because Cash's ex-partner, Sam Beaujolais, was on vacation and couldn't take her call. As near as Marley could tell, everyone adored Cash.

Annie Dean had returned Marley's previous call, and while she'd seemed suspicious of Marley's story— Marley said she was a New York lifestyles writer interested in covering Bourbon Street's nightlife—the manager had confirmed that Cash owned the Cash Cow, which was all Marley had wanted to know.

Despite the shake-up at the Darden's yesterday morning, all Marley's suspicions seemed silly now. *A cop*, she thought again. She felt as if a veil had been removed, exposing her for the worrisome idiot she'd become since Chris had left. Not that she was going to beat herself up about that, either. She'd worked so hard, not only at her business, but trying to forge a relationship that would last, one that mirrored the closeness her own folks shared. She'd hoped she and Chris could start a family....

"Here," someone said, breaking her reverie. "Cash is on his way out, Edie, and we need to touch up your eye makeup. It's melting under the lights. Don't worry about getting your face wet. Everything's waterproof."

Dutifully, she raised her chin, sighing as she remembered once more how hard she'd worked to build Fancy Abs. Maybe because she was a twin, she'd wanted to build something all her own, and while Chris had known about the deeper significance she'd attached to her business, that hadn't stopped him from taking money she'd saved for a key expansion. Seeing his self-centeredness hurt more than anything. Besides, whatever success she'd had was for their future. As a tennis instructor, Chris was never going to earn as much as her. Only after their marriage had she realized he never would have become a full partner. For the rest of her life, she'd have been the one to carry the ball....

Trying to forget, Marley took a deep breath. A year had passed since the divorce papers were final, and she couldn't live the rest of her life projecting distrustful feelings onto men who deserved better, such as Cash.

After getting his start in the bar business as a bouncer, Cash had decided to move from doorman security into law enforcement, only to transition back into the restaurant-bar industry after finishing the academy and working as a cop—this time as his own boss, calling the shots, using the money he'd earned at the NOPD to live his dream of opening his own club. Where he'd seemed shifty before, it was becoming increasingly clear that he was far more successful than she'd imagined and that he had a lot of irons in the fire.

She'd also realized that if he wasn't on the level, *Rate the Dates* would have exposed him by now. Their interview over the phone with Edie had included questions about Edie's background, and Edie had told Marley that they'd checked out her answers. Surely, they'd done the same for Cash. Not that *Rate the Dates* knew everything, of course, seeing as Marley was impersonating Edie....

Put the past to rest, she schooled herself. Obviously, the warning signals she'd received regarding Cash weren't on the mark. And maybe the protective expression in his eyes at the Dardens had done something to further warm her. Surely, Edie was right, and the breakup with Marley's ex was interfering with her radar again. That, or how Granny Ginny's impending visit had reminded her of the bad dates that seemed to substantiate the idea that she and her sisters really were cursed.

"You can open your eyes now," said a makeup artist.

When Marley did, the vision in front of her nearly made her heart cease beating. "Wow," she whispered hoarsely. Cash was standing at the edge of the Jacuzzi in a black swimsuit that left absolutely nothing to the imagination. The makeup artists had proven their talents once more and covered the scratch on his cheek.

One of the female technicians wolf whistled and jokingly said, "Maybe I'll go on *Rate the Dates*."

From Marley's vantage point, seated on a step and submerged to her neck in bubbling water, Cash looked ten rather than six feet tall. And dark. He had the kind of tan that came from living in the South for years. It had turned all the usually covered parts of him a deep chestnut brown.

His body was everything she'd imagined, but it was always hard to gauge the exact offerings until a man took off his clothes. With Cash, she might have experienced distrust, but in the physical arena, she felt nothing but desire. He was covered with lots of hair, but not too much, just enough to make him look dangerously animal, and as his run through the woods at the Dardens had proven, he could move like a jungle cat, largely due to muscles now visibly evident. Thick between his pectorals, all that luscious hair was wavy and black, and Marley inhaled audibly as her eyes followed the thinning, swirling line of it down between his ribs.

It was the wrong time for a technician, who was explaining how to work the Jacuzzi controls, to turn knobs that increased heat and pressure, sending hot bubbles between her legs. Uttering a jagged breath, she glanced quickly upward, into Cash's eyes. He was staring down, hardly listening to the technician any more than she, and checking out her suit.

His smiled melted her wherever the hot water hadn't, and she sank another inch under the water, feeling ripples buffet her as he began stepping into the pool. She took in each inch of him as he moved, from his well-shaped feet, to his legs, which were just as she liked them—long, bunched with muscle and coated with springy black hairs. Her heart skittered as her eyes landed on the tight, clingy black suit. She could make out the entire shape of him, the tempting thickness and delineated ridges....

"Very fine," she whispered under her breath.

The technician was saying, "Now, don't get embarrassed. We cameramen do this all the time. Act as natural as possible, even though the cameras are on. This isn't being aired live, so if you get too aroused, the studio can edit for whatever segments they replay when we're on live tonight."

As Cash sank into the four-foot pool, he smiled and said, "That's good to know," as if he had every intention of becoming very aroused.

The technician spun the dial again, saying, "There. We want some wild water. Something viewers can see, so give us some nice romance."

She was swallowing hard, heat suffusing her body from both the increased water temperature and the fact that Cash was drifting toward her, when the technician reminded, "You've got an open bottle of bubbly beside you and two full glasses. Lets see what you can do with it."

As he'd been instructed, Cash pretended he didn't even notice the cameras were there. Slowly, he floated toward her, looking completely weightless; foaming water lapped at his hair, taming waving ends that were the color of midnight. "Nice suit," he murmured, his fingers splaying beneath the water, reaching for her. As they curled around her feet, stroking the insteps, she sucked in a shaky breath.

"Your suit's not bad, either," she pointed out, lifting her voice, knowing the microphones were picking up everything.

Now, completely breaking the rules, Cash stared directly into the camera lens, offering a crocodile grin. "I thought she'd like it."

She laughed. "I don't usually get to see so much of a man in winter."

"You ought to see what I wear in summer."

She eyed him. "You wear less than this?"

"Stick around and find out." Gliding his hands upward on her bare legs, he solicited a sharp intake of breath as he parted them. He glided between her legs then and reached past her head. As he urged her thighs to lock around his hips, he lifted a glass of champagne, took a sip, then handed it to her.

As she took it, he slid a finger under the shoulder strap of the suit, tracing the area and exploring her collarbone, his palm coming to rest on her chest, the heel of it just touching the swell of a breast. "Nice," he whispered, dropping a searing gaze to her cleavage. "I've got lots of questions about this suit, staring with, how does it stay on?"

Tilting her chin downward, so it touched the rim of the glass, she surveyed him. "Maybe it doesn't."

His eyes glinted with amusement, and when he spoke, the sugary cadence of his speech turned the moment heavier, weighing it down, the way moss pulled down cypress branches in the bayous where he spent his free time fishing. "If the cameras weren't on, would you take this off for me, Mar..." His eyes widening with surprise, he stopped himself and finished, saying, "Edie."

Marley's face faltered. She really did hate being called by her sister's name. Suddenly, she wished the charade was over. All her life, she and her twin had tried to differentiate themselves. And here she was, with this hot man, who was calling her Edie. "Why don't you call me sweetheart," she suggested, trying—and failing—to keep her tone upbeat, as if they were merely amusing themselves with a little verbal sparring, which they weren't. "Or darling." Anything but Edie.

"All right," he said huskily, the expression of his eyes deepening, as if he understood fully why she'd made the request. "But you didn't answer my question."

"If I was alone, would I take it off for you?"

He nodded. Was he playing for the cameras? Or was he serious about them sleeping together? Sure, they wanted each other. Some of their kisses had been real scorchers, and yesterday in the truck, they'd wrestled enough that he'd gotten fully aroused. It had felt good, too, she thought as another rush of heat infused her body. Were they prepared to go for it, though? With him watching her so intently, she felt exposed and raw. "I wish the cameras weren't on," she admitted in a whisper.

"I'm going to take that as a yes."

Maybe he should. It was inadvisable, and definitely not in keeping with her New Year's resolution, but Marley wanted him. The curse would, no doubt, throw her some extra curveball if she followed her desire. Still, she trusted him enough now, ever since she'd found out about his background as a cop. She let him take the champagne, her body moving with his as he took a sip and glided closer, landing her right in front of the water jets. When he heard her gasp, he said, "What?"

As if he didn't know. The male part of him had just settled against her, making her feel jittery and confused about what they were doing exactly. The cameras were rolling! Butterflies took flight in her belly as he tilted the champagne glass to her lips. "Another sip?" he murmured.

"Sure."

Sweet effervescent taste burst in her mouth, and as she swallowed, letting him hold the glass for her, she thought, all this is happening so fast. Under the water, his hips eddied against hers. Soaked with water, already thin material clung to their skin, and the longer the ridge of him pressured her, the more she had to fight a very pleasurable drowning sensation. "It just that—" she began again, "—this doesn't feel like a game, anymore, Cash."

"It's as real as we want to make it."

Her wet arms slid around his neck; their bellies

collided, and the tips of her breasts beaded almost painfully, aching for him. She bit back a soft cry when their nipples actually brushed, with nothing but a scant scrap of string between them.

"Real?" she managed to say. They were on TV, and she was supposed to be Edie. Behind his back, she'd been playing detective, checking out the claims he made about himself as if she were Miss Marple. And yet the energy between them was unstoppable. Ever since she'd talked to Annie Dean and called the New Orleans Police Department, a weight had been lifted from her. Floodgates had opened. Sure, she was still worried about the danger at the Dardens', but that had nothing to do with Cash. Probably, all her suspicious feelings were entirely ungrounded. She was acting like an idiot.

Of course she was, she suddenly thought. How many women in this situation wouldn't act crazy? His eyes held hers as if they'd never let go. Narrowing to slits, they almost shut as he angled his head and offered a thorough kiss that pushed darker heat through her limbs. All the world was watching, but the kiss crowded out any perception of that. As he drew away, he said, "Sweetheart, our kisses make us winners. I'll be happy to walk off this show. Right now. This very minute. Just say the word."

She couldn't help but smile. "You'd leave the show just to prove you don't care about winning?"

His fingers splayed on either side of her spine. Using them, he drew her closer, tightening the embrace. "Romance with you is my only concern."

He looked absolutely sincere. As he turned their bodies in the water and floated her backwards, she realized that he knew just exactly where those water jets were positioned. He must have listened to the technician more than he'd let on. Bubbles frothed between her legs and his eyes smoldered. She knew she'd better not move because the cameras were on her face. He was responding, too, getting firmer, pressing harder. Those jets pounded now, the pulsing massage threatening to send her over the top. "I can think of a hundred things I'd like to do to you," she found herself murmuring, "and I can't do even one of them."

"Your plans for me are that X-rated?"

"Yes," she whispered simply, knowing the studio audience would eat this up, and yet not caring, knowing that wasn't the point of her saying the words.

His lips were a relief. Feeling them firmly fasten to hers, she parted for him, letting the kiss swallow her whimper. No sound escaped, but only because he was expertly probing her with his tongue—using the tip to tease her teeth before starting to stroke inside her cheek....

Everything went black as she let sensation claim her. She was teetering in the abyss, everything unbearable now—the heat of his erection, the force of his tongue. And then somebody shouted, "Good job. That's a wrap, folks."

WHEN CASH SUGGESTED they go to his hotel, Marley hadn't expected it to be the Four Seasons, nor for the room to be quite so nice. In fact, it was classy enough that no one in the lobby had glanced at her even though she was outfitted in the sweatpants she'd worn to the Dardens' and hardly looked like a Four Seasons regular. There'd been no time to change before going to the studio, not that Marley had gotten particularly mussed this morning. After yesterday, it was determined that Julia's workouts would take place inside until the attacker was caught.

Marley wished she'd had a chance to talk about the near-shooting with both Cash and Edie, but to do so she'd needed privacy, since such matters concerning the Dardens weren't to be made public. Besides, there hadn't been time; Edie had gotten through to Marley's cell, but Marley had been busy talking to Miranda. After taping in the Jacuzzi, time was equally rushed since Marley and Cash had been marshaled into separate dressing rooms. Moments later they were wearing sports gear and, after playing indoor golf, during which Cash had flirted mercilessly, further distracting her, they'd been escorted to a rehearsal session for the movie premiere before going on the air. Now it was ten o'clock.

"Here." He lifted a down jacket from her shoulders, placing it on a chair. After flicking off the overhead light in favor of the muted glow of a bedside lamp, he turned on a radio tuned to blues. "Should I order some food?"

"Maybe more champagne," Marley managed to say, feeling hungry, but so nervous she wasn't sure she could eat. She hated the feeling; she was used to being self-starting and in control, something Chris had seen as a character deficit. Eyeing Cash, she realized that in a long-term, serious relationship, he'd probably be the type to want an equal partner.

"That you've got," he said.

"Oh." She suddenly laughed, realizing she'd been lost in thought. "I get it. Champagne. As in Cash."

She glanced around an airy room decorated mostly in white, with a chalky duvet and milky window sheers. The only color was from mixed tropical flowers that burst from a red vase on a table, looking shocking in the muted ambiance. Taking off his coat and sport jacket, he stripped to a soft chambray shirt he was wearing tucked into jeans and shot her a slow smile. "At the moment, you're not your usual quick self, Marley. What were you thinking?"

"That you'd never get along with a woman you could control."

"Women like that bore me," he said easily. Seemingly registering her anxious expression, he added, "Are you okay?"

"Not really. Uh…I think we're about to have sex."

He studied her a moment. "We don't have to."

She stared back, making him smile by saying, "Uh…yes we do." And it was true. Neither of them would sleep until they'd satisfied their curiosity. After tucking a fallen lock of hair behind her ear, she tightened the band that held the rest of it back, away from her face. "I'm just nervous."

"Me, too." His eyes went still, penetrating hers as he lifted the receiver to call room service.

Maybe. But Marley didn't really think Cash looked all *that* nervous. "It must be performance anxiety," she said, trying to make light.

As he waited for room service to pick up, he pinned her with his gaze, his dark eyes sparkling. "Yours or mine?"

She dropped her jaw. "Yours, of course."

His laugh tempered to a chuckle, his teeth flashing bone-white in the dim light. He drawled, "Let me get this straight. You're afraid you're going to regret the best sex of your life."

"You really do have a high opinion of yourself."

"True," he offered, still grinning. "But it's earned."

Like trust, she couldn't help but think. Silence fell, and the tension in the room suddenly seemed palpable, making Marley wish that everything was over and done with. She'd like to fast-forward, through all the groping and divesting of clothes. Truly, there was nothing worse than first-time sex, she thought. "Don't you kind of wish we'd already done it?" she couldn't help but say.

Obviously, he didn't have a clue what she meant. "Huh?"

"Avoiding the first time is the thing I most liked about being married," she admitted.

"You liked getting used to a steady partner?"

Nodding, she was glad he understood now. In committed relationships, you learned what he liked. He learned what you liked. It had made everything so easy. And effective. She'd been able to relax and enjoy herself....

"Don't worry, Marley." Another peal of soft, lazy laughter floated to her ears. "We can shut our eyes, go real fast and pretend it's not even happening, okay?"

That made her grin. She watched as he turned his attention to the phone; she'd almost forgotten he was on hold, waiting for room service. After he ordered, he hung up, saying, "They'll be right up with champagne."

She managed a nod, wishing her heart wasn't beating wildly in her chest. "The room's nice."

After glancing toward the king-size bed, he simply crossed to her side, took her hand and drawled in a hoarse voice that threatened to thoroughly undo her, "Let's make ourselves comfortable."

A moment later, he'd drawn back the duvet, and they were lying on their sides on the mattress, face to face, their heads resting on huge pillows covered in Egyptian cotton. "What should we do until champagne comes?" she whispered.

"The champagne's here, sweetheart."

This time, she got it. "You can call me Marley now." For hours, she'd been called by her sister's name, and now she wanted to hear her own.

Right before his lips pressed to hers, feeling firm and cool from the winter air, he whispered back, "Marley." Shuddering, knowing where this kiss was going to lead, she glided a hand down his side. The chambray shirt was warm and inviting, floating under her fingers like water, but not feeling nearly as interesting as the skin she found near his wrist. His pulse was beating every bit as hard as hers. "I bet we're going to be pretty hot together, Cash Champagne."

"That's a good bet," he agreed, his own hand mimicking the motions of hers, stroking her side. Molding his hand over her hip, he tested the curve, then he moaned softly as he cupped the flesh of her backside, urging her to him. Their hips connected, and when she felt him nestling where her thighs met, she gasped.

His mouth descended, and as his tongue lapped against hers, fingers began exploring the sides of her breasts, the caresses drawing sounds of pleasure from her. He filled his hands, making her glad she'd foregone the confining sports bra she'd worn earlier. The cotton of a long-sleeved T-shirt was no barrier, and the sensations wrought by those huge hands enveloping her breasts rocked her, making her shiver. "It's been a long time…" she whispered, her voice trailing off.

"Let's make up for it," he said huskily.

After offering gentle squeezes that shot to her core, he pulled harder, tweaking her nipples, engendering pangs so strong that she couldn't believe the hands were on her upper body, not lower….

So much lower…

Deepening the kiss, she tussled with her tongue, wrestling for control while he teased her nipples through her clothes, drawing them between fingers and thumbs. Using his nails, he flicked the buds, then tugged lightly again, igniting her, making her pulse skyrocket. "I didn't trust you at first," she murmured, her voice hitching.

His eyes seemed veiled, hard to read. "But now?"

Whimpering between kisses that were turning wetter and more languid, she felt crazy, unnameable things call out inside her. "I…trust you enough."

"Enough?"

"For this," she murmured. "For tonight." Shuddering as his thumbs circled taut buds again, she felt heat jag inside her. Bright and fast, it exploded as his touch turned rougher, and he pushed his tongue deeper.

"Enough for this?" he said, his drawl a rasp in his throat, his hips suddenly rolling, grinding insistently against her, pushing her toward ecstasy. "And for this," he murmured, plucking the tips of her breasts until they started to ache and burn. Her belly felt strangely full to bursting as her hips rose, arching, the sensations inside her reaching upward in dazzling spirals, climbing…

Just as a knock sounded at the door, he rolled on the mattress, hauling her beneath him, and she found herself reaching up, grabbing his shirttails and opening the pearl-studded snaps in a gesture, then pushing the fabric over bare shoulders that were even more silken, exposing a hairy chestnut-colored chest that burned with fever as the shirt fell away. Pungent scent burst between them, the smell of need rising between their bodies and hitting her nostrils like an airborne aphrodisiac.

"Be right back," he murmured. She nodded as he rose, stopping in the bathroom to get some condoms, she realized, and then answering the door for room service. Not letting the server wheel inside with the tray, he took the glasses and bottle, scribbled his signature and gently kicked shut the door.

"Now," he said, returning to the bedside, uncorking the bottle and pouring the glasses. "We can really get started."

Her voice was deep, throaty. "I thought we already did."

When Cash slowly shook his head, she couldn't even muster a smile. "Champagne?" he asked, lifting a glass.

She shook her head, grabbed his hand and pulled him back into bed on top of her. "This is all the Champagne I want."

"Here's to you," he whispered, his eyes drinking her in as he placed his elbows on either side of her head. Reaching, he found the band that held her hair and eased it from wavy strands, releasing them so they fell around her shoulders. Taking a deep breath, he toyed with the tendrils, catching them between splayed fingers, brushing them away from her face and over the pillow. Not to be outdone, she lifted both hands, and began teasing his nipples, just as he'd done to her, and she watched with pleasure as his jaw slackened. Dark shadows of lust appeared in his eyes, making the irises look glossy.

He was so hard between her legs. She could feel him rigid and tight, bursting with need. Cash lowered his mouth once more, and in another heartbeat, they were loving each other, rolling as they undressed, their hands hungry. Unleashing the tie to her pants, he pushed them over her hips, down her legs and to the floor, leaving her panties. He took off his jeans, his briefs. As she veered back, lifting the shirt over her head, her breasts swung free, and the eyes that landed on them were as greedy as hands that reached as he whispered, "Marley."

His mouth found her in a splash of scalding liquid that covered a nipple, squirting fire through her body while a splayed hand rubbed her bare belly, moving lower to strip down her panties, another gliding upward to capture a bare breast. Crying out, her hips arched once more, seeking him even as her hands reached down to close over his straining length. As she fisted fingers around him, he breathed in sharply, and at the sound of need, darkness descended.

She wanted…everything. She wanted…to hear

him gasp more as she stroked him, and he did, in a stream of needy nonsensical sounds as she kept gliding her hand along the burning shaft.

"Marley," he muttered. "Sweetheart. Oh."

Squeezing, she reveled in the feel of him, each ridge, the silken head, her own internal senses peaking as his lips locked hard to her breast again, taking her deeper into pleasure, nearer to orgasm, his tongue swirling in maddening circles. She wanted… this fire, this heat. To feel him come inside her, and to watch his face when he lost his reason. With each new fisted stroke, she felt his erection strengthen and passion rushed through her, heating her veins….

She wanted to tell him she was soaked, gushing because of what he was doing to her, but she moaned instead, melting as the searing damp pad of his tongue flickered fast against a bud. Torturous, excruciating heat poured through her, making her cry out, her core disintegrating. Her mind went blank, as that wet spear dropped into her cleavage, spun in lazy spirals and trailed to her belly, his fingers twining in her pubic hair now, tugging gently….

Her thigh slammed him where he ached, and he muttered a soft curse right before his head ducked. She panted hard, the breasts he'd moistened bereft, the dark stubble of his chin raking her thighs, the rasping, wild curly hairs of his chest brushing her legs. His mouth covered her core, settled there, rested a moment in a heaven of liquid fire.

She parted more…more. She'd never been so open to a man, and when he ceased pleasuring her and left her dangling over the precipice, she could only stare down at his wild dark hair, her eyes glazed. Vaguely, she was aware of the sculpted muscles in the arms that supported him. Locks of dark tangled hair fell into his eyes when he glanced up to her face, and in the low light, his chest and shoulders glowed with inner fire.

His hands found her shoulders, and her heart swelled as she cupped her hand around his nape, gently now, her fingers trembling, urging him nearer, shuddering when his bald erection touched her swimming heat.

"Wait a minute," he whispered, his voice strangled. Reaching for the bedside table, he found a condom, ripped the foil with his teeth and sheathed himself.

"The teeth," she whispered, barely recognizing her own voice, which was husky with desire. "Very macho."

He managed a smile. "Thought you'd like that maneuver."

"It adds that extra touch," she murmured.

And then he was simply staring into her eyes again. His voice was straining with more tenderness than she'd imagined him capable of. "I'm glad we're doing this, Marley."

Everything inside her felt more alive than she'd imagined was possible. When he rested a quivering palm on her thigh, she parted, her whole body flushing as she guided him in. Drawing a breath through his teeth, he filled her, sighing as a cry of need was drawn from her.

The kiss was no longer a kiss, only open-mouthed contact as he pushed all the way in—deep, deeper, deepest. Uttering a soft cry, she circled both arms tightly around his neck as he dragged her down, beneath him, grasping her hips as he thrust. Her mind awash in a landscape of passionate darkness, Marley let him take control, filling her. She had no idea what this lovemaking meant, if there would be a future for them, or if they'd win a grand prize, or be thwarted by an old family curse that Cash Champagne was making her start to disbelieve again.

And at the moment, Marley didn't care in the least. The moment was more than enough. Tightening her arms around him, she clung and felt only the pleasure.

7

"THAT WAS…" MARLEY WHISPERED hours later, searching for a word.

Absently stroking her hair, Cash merely nodded, murmuring, "No need to put a name on it." And yet he could think of countless words. Amazing. Mindblowing. Unexpected. But any way he cut it, he was mentally kicking himself now. He'd been so close to resolving so many things in his life, but sex with Marley had seriously complicated matters.

He'd had women before. More than his share. For better or worse, it came with the job of being a big-city club owner, but Marley was different, and the energy between them couldn't be explained away with words such as lust or desire. This was deeper, fueled by something trickier that nobody on earth had ever really found a usable name for. Emotions, some said. Chemistry. Fate.

Whatever it was, common sense should have made Cash steer clear of it. She was lying so very still on top of him, her breath shallow as if she were sleeping, and her flattened palms and face were resting on his chest. Her cheek brushed his chest hairs, and the top of her head touched his chin. Every time he breathed, he inhaled the sweet smell of her hair, making him ache to be inside her again even though he was spent. He felt like an addict with a drug—one time wasn't going to be enough. He'd known better than to taste of the fruit, but now it was too late. Gazing down, he exhaled such a heartfelt sigh that she murmured, "What?"

"I'm just sleepy."

He wasn't, of course. Just furious with himself. When he'd come to New York a month ago, he'd had unshakable plans, all of which were so inadvisable that he'd lied to everyone. No one knew he was here. His ex-partner, Sam Beaujolais, had even made him vow he wouldn't come. And Annie Dean thought he'd left town to do some business, then go on a fishing trip with Sam. He could only hope the two didn't happen to run into each other, although they probably wouldn't, since Sam was on vacation himself for a couple more days.

None of his friends would believe he was in bed with a Benning. Oh, he'd meant to meet one. Maybe even date one. But now...

He tried to push away mixed feelings, knowing he couldn't afford emotions. They were a luxury, and when he'd come North this time, he'd known he had to keep a clear head. Nothing could threaten to undermine him. Shaking his head in disgust, he wondered what he was supposed to do now. Get up and leave? Even if he wanted to do so, could he?

Doubtful, he decided, his throat closing as he stroked the hair spread across his chest and registered the warmth where their bodies met from their chests to their toes. For one insane moment, he actually considered telling her everything, but he knew she'd only hate him.

Wondering if he'd left anything incriminating in sight, he glanced around the room, decided he hadn't, then shifted his gaze to the window. Heavier drapes were pushed to the sides, and since they were on an upper floor, with no buildings opposite, Cash had used only the sheers to veil the night. Stars glistened, shining through the filmy fabric, making him feel that he and Marley had ascended into their own heaven and were floating high above the world.

The thought almost made him smile. His ex-partner, Sam, had always said Cash was too sensitive to be a cop. It was a standard joke between them, since both men prided themselves on being tough.

"Sensitive," Cash would counter. "Never."

Sam would stare at him a long moment and say, "You are so, Cash. Deep down. Where a man starts to be human." He'd say it as if Cash were a stranger to human feeling.

But tonight, Marley had touched that core place.

"What?" she murmured again, as if sensing his thoughts were about her. He continued brushing her hair with his fingers, twirling the tendrils at the roots. "You make me think poetic thoughts, Marley Benning," he admitted.

"I'll call you Frost," she whispered in sleepy promise, her voice sounding dreamy. "Or maybe Housman. Or Eliot."

"You know a lot of poets for a fitness instructor."

"If you recognized the names, then you know a lot of poets for an ex-cop." She shrugged. "Anyway, Edie reads them. She's the romantic."

"You don't do so bad with romance, yourself."

"No one in my family would believe you."

He could only shake his head. "Do you really believe you and your sisters are cursed when it comes to romance?" he found himself saying, his own heart suddenly twisting, leaving him to wonder whether he'd be one more man who proved them right.

She rolled to the side, stretching her naked body down the length of his, and his whole body felt bereft until she cuddled, snuggling her face into the hollow of his shoulder. Realizing his eyes could feast on her again, he let them. Changing the subject, he whispered, "That's the great thing about fitness instructors."

"What?"

"Great bodies."

Her blue eyes were just smoky slits. She smiled up at him. "You should have seen it before I started eating junk food."

His gaze dropped over her—the disheveled mass of hair that fell around her like a waterfall, the skin that she kept more hydrated than a supermodel's, her ripe breasts that tasted tangier than any fresh fruit. "I don't think I could have handled you before."

She looked pleased. "Probably not, Cash."

He adjusted the sheet over them. Her skin was clammy now, warm and girlish, and as he hugged her close, he realized he needed to get some sleep. "I take it you're spending the night."

She shut her eyes, nodding. "Do you want me to leave?"

"No."

And yet, a part of him didn't want her to stay, either. After tonight, he knew he wouldn't keep his hands off her. He should have done so. He knew that now. But he'd had no idea she'd affect him like this.

Even worse, this incredible lovemaking had happened in New York. There was nowhere on earth Cash hated more, probably because his last trip here had been such a disaster. He'd felt put off by all the usual things. The dirt and crime. For a couple days, he'd wandered the streets in a fog. He'd watched tourists with too much money to burn traipsing from Broadway shows and fancy hotels, talking too loudly and flaunting expensive finery while stretch limos, as dark and shiny as the night, had glided down wide avenues, their windows tinted, hiding the wealthy from view as they passed homeless people sleeping on the subway grates. Cash hated that kind of decadence. And the noise. The horns and sirens had driven him crazy. He'd been eaten up with fury on the last night he'd spent here, desperate to avenge himself on the person he'd come to hurt....

A man he'd almost killed.

Now he shuddered to think of what could have happened to him. His whole life could have ended on his last night here. In fact, it almost had. When the man he'd most hated had shown him mercy, he'd fled. It had been the lowest blow, the thing hardest to take.

New Orleans had opened her loving arms again, though. The crescent city of his birth was a beacon of light after New York's enveloping darkness. His first time out of the Deep South, he'd had eyes that were long accustomed to trailing flowers growing on pink-and-white stucco, so he'd been stunned by the ugly gray skyscrapers, his vision stunted by a landscape that seemed stark and dismal.

He'd never been so glad for the bustle of French

Quarter markets, or the hominess of the precinct. For three days, he'd simply walked the streets he'd known since birth, feeling as if he'd never seen them before, stopping in countless bars where he could get a beer and where everybody knew his name. Listening to blues wailing from open doorways, he'd stare at women smiling down at him from wrought-iron balconies as if they were a novelty, and every night, he'd bury himself in another set of warm, sultry arms, hoping he'd find the one woman who could take away the New York chill still running in his veins.

He never did. Maybe not until tonight with Marley Benning. He'd spent three miserable days that way, in a haze of booze, fury and raw sex that, deep down, he knew wouldn't do a damn thing to appease the pain inside him.

And then Cash Champagne had finally buried his mother.

Suddenly, he startled, hearing Marley stir beside him. He'd thought she'd fallen asleep. "Do you want to go over to my folks' apartment for breakfast? Maybe meet my Granny Ginny?"

He glanced down just as she yawned. Her eyes opened, looking dreamy, like fog on a morning ocean. Since he'd been thinking of his own family, he was jarred by the question. "Breakfast?"

"Yeah. Edie will be there," warned Marley, oblivious of his thoughts. "And Bridget. Have you met Bridget?"

He nodded, thinking of her youngest sister. "Once."

Nodding, she said, "Mom was watching the first show, and she saw us kissing..."

"So, she wants me to come over for breakfast?"

"Dinner's not good right now, because of the show. And Julia canceled our workout session day after tomorrow, since she's got a hair appointment, and Mom had already asked me over, since Granny Ginny's here, so…"

Marley thought it might be a good time for him to meet her family. Maybe it no longer mattered, he thought. Everything had veered so far off course from his original plans that right now, nothing seemed redeemable. "You don't have to," she said quickly, but he could hear the hurt.

"It's not that I don't want to," he began diplomatically.

"What then?"

"Well…maybe it is," he amended, still stroking her hair. "I just realized…I guess I've gotten to you, Marley, just the way you've gotten to me, which means we're both already exactly where we didn't want to be."

She glanced up, curious. "Where's that?"

"Where we can both get hurt."

"Good point. So, let's nix the breakfast."

Now it was his turn to feel disappointed. No doubt, this whole thing would blow up in his face. She was going to wind up hating him. She was going to get hurt. Whatever fantasy she was building in her mind about who he was would disintegrate at some point, and blow away like dust, and he'd wind up fulfilling the Benning family prophecy about all the sisters being old maids. Still, he couldn't walk away from her. "Okay," he countered against his own best judgement. "Why not?"

"Because you might have a good time. And then you might want more sex with me. And then you might come to care for me...."

She had a point there. "I already want more sex with you."

She giggled. "When?"

"I thought you were going to sleep."

Before she stretched her arms around his neck and drew him into an embrace, she said, "Not without a nightcap, Cash."

"That's why I ordered you that champagne," he reminded her.

"I want this Champagne instead," she said.

"ARE WE ABOUT READY TO GO?" Marley asked a couple days later as Cash braced himself, preparing to meet her folks.

"Almost." As Marley put on her coat, Cash paid the check and glanced around at the early morning crowd in the Riviera on Seventh Avenue where they'd stopped for coffee, then he returned his gaze to Marley, barely able to believe the unmistakable fact that he was falling for her. And in only five days.

It had been a whirlwind—from the first night when they'd wound up on TV, to their dinner at Alexandria's, to their first night in bed. They'd been taped while skating, golfing and making out in a hot tub. Last night, they'd gone to a premiere, where they'd glimpsed stars they'd seen in movies, and although she'd been embarrassed, Cash had urged Marley to meet her favorites, even getting her an autograph from Tom Cruise. After the show her parents had called to ask for details, not appeased until Cash had gotten on the phone, making small talk with both Viv and Joe Benning, both of whom kept saying they were looking forward to meeting him at breakfast this morning.

"We put on quite a show this week," Marley said. "Do you think we'll win?"

He lowered his chin and kissed her, his mind fogging to gray at the touch of their lips. "No show, Marley. I really like you." Leaning away and folding a copy of the *Times,* he tucked it under his arm, then lifted his espresso and knocked back another sip. He felt drowsy from ravishing her body at the hotel after they'd awakened. Last night, which they'd spent together, had been even better than the night before.

The after-tingle put a smile on his face. "You'll have to forgive me. I'm moving a little slow this morning."

"I wore you out?"

He laughed. "Do you really expect me to feed your ego?"

"Sure. Or I might feel compelled to find another man."

"I hope not," he said, polishing off the last of the espresso. "That's another thing I'll give you—" Rising and offering his hand, he decided he liked how Marley's company had tempered his previously negative feelings toward the city. "The coffee's almost as good as what we have in the Quarter."

"Maybe," she countered as they headed toward the door, "but our newspapers are better."

"I'd heard New Yorkers were snobs."

"We do like the best of everything," she assured, her eyes drifting pointedly over his body as he opened the door. A brisk wind hit them, and once outside, he realized a light snow had begun to fall, dusting the pavement, making it glitter. How could he have thought New York ugly? Sure, the day was overcast, but the air was charged, the gray sky kinetic, energized by people bustling through it.

She said, "You look nice, Cash."

"Thanks." He was keeping plenty of secrets from her, the least of which concerned the extra time he'd spent dressing this morning. Because of his growing feelings for her, he'd given himself a closer-than-average shave and tucked a crisp white shirt into the dress slacks he'd packed to wear to business meetings.

While dating Edie, he'd avoided the other Bennings. How he felt about Marley was so different. Edie was soft, where Marley was hard. Slow, where Marley was fast. Predictably romantic, where Marley was inventive. Edie was the kind of woman who worried over details that Cash called minutiae and who stopped to pet every mangy dog in the street, neither of which was Marley's style.

He'd been using Edie, plain and simple, and both of them had been mortified at their few attempted kisses. Kissing Marley was a whole other story. Once more, he wondered if they were going to win tonight on *Rate the Dates*, and he realized that, either way, he'd be satisfied because he intended to ask Marley to come back to the Four Seasons again after the show.

"You look nice, too," he said now. Cash had only seen Marley wear sweatpants, Edie's suit and the clothes chosen by the *Rate the Dates* staff, but Marley's closet did have other offerings. The black pants suit she'd chosen was chic, and she'd worn her hair loose and wild, the way he liked it. Her favorite down jacket had been replaced by an ankle-length black wool coat with an open seam at the back, which made the ends blow in the wind. "Very dramatic."

She smiled. "Thanks."

Wrapping an arm around her shoulders, he drew her close, no longer surprised to feel how perfectly she fit against his side, or how their strides matched. Their first night together in bed had ended any pretense of trying to keep their hands off each other, and during their second night, last night, they'd shared a bubble bath, as well as invented some interesting games with deserts ordered from room service.

"I can hardly believe the week's over," he murmured, kissing the top of her head. Or that he was glad about it. "After this evening, when we win on *Rate the Dates*, you're all mine, Marley Benning."

"And to think, on New Year's, I'd sworn off men."

When she smiled at him, he felt an uncharacteristic surge of caring warmth and in response, he started to remind her that it was cold out, and she should have worn a hat, but he didn't, and he was glad about that, too. She looked gorgeous without one. Flaxen strands of hair teased his lips, reminding him of how she'd looked an hour ago, too, lying naked atop the duvet on her belly, her legs crooked. Now he sucked in a sharp breath, pulling biting air into his lungs, recalling how he'd joined her in bed, gliding his palms over her bare backside, slowly caressing the flesh before entering her from behind.

Passion flooded him at the memory, and he had to wonder where this was headed. Was he just deluding himself? Was this just one more chimera related to their being on the show, as she sometimes suggested? And yet the lure of winning fast cash meant nothing to him....

About his hidden agenda, he was more confused. At any rate, he'd wrapped up his legitimate business in town. Not for the first time, he stood to make a killing. As for the other pressing matter in his life, he was still stymied. Every step forward was a reminder that he was using Marley, just as he'd started to use her sister.

He blew out a sigh. Even after all these years, Cash could work himself into a fit of blind anger when he thought of the past. He'd been wronged beyond what a man could endure. Forced to live a lie. In just one day, years ago, he'd lost everything he'd ever lived for. Someone might as well have taken away his personality, his name. In a sense they had. Sometimes, he'd felt as if someone had reached deep inside him and simply ripped out the core of his soul. He'd felt aimless after that. Lost. Like half a man.

And yet, with Marley walking beside him now, Cash also felt...happy. The past was inconsequential shadows, nothing more. Day had broken. Or at least he had glimpses through the clouds of anger he carried inside him. At such moments, his own thinking, his desire for revenge, seemed twisted to him, and vaguely, he wondered if the events of his own life were even true. Had he really almost killed a man? Sometimes, when he looked at Marley Benning, such a thing seemed impossible....

He took in the waves tangling around her face, eyeing strands that were the color of sunlit wheat, and his heart swelled. His lips parted, and he started to tell her why he'd really come here, that he'd meant to use the Benning women, only to have Marley begin to change him in only a few days.

He wanted her forgiveness. But to get it, she'd have to know the truth. And he could imagine how her eyes would look if he told her. They'd swim in dark shadows, filled with the betrayal she'd experienced when her husband left…a betrayal from which she felt Cash was helping her heal, at least until she realized the truth—he was as bad as the man she'd married….

It didn't take an expert on human emotion to anticipate her expression of wounded injury. Lips that were smiling now, glossed lips that had kissed every inch of him, would part in shock. But Marley wouldn't cry. At least not for a long time. No, she'd get furious at him first, just the way he would in similar circumstances. They had that in common.

He wouldn't stick around. That's how he imagined the breakup. Maybe she'd softened him enough that he wouldn't pursue unfinished business here. He'd simply let sleeping dogs lie, and go back to New Orleans before everything hit the fan with Marley. But then, he'd feel like a coward. Because he'd be walking out on something he wanted more than he'd wanted anything in a long time—her.

Now she shivered, pulling him from his reverie, and as she stretched her arm around him, pocketing her gloved hand inside his coat, he found her long fingers and twined them through his. It looked as if they were going to win on *Rate the Dates.* Maybe he'd give her his share of the prize money, he thought, then he realized his motive was guilt over using her.

"I was thinking you could start another club with the money if we win," he found himself suggesting, "the way you've been planning."

Her voice caught. "I hope so."

"Got any names for it?"

"Fancy Abs would appeal to old clients of mine, but I want a fresh start. A new name. New location."

How new? The thought came unbidden. He tried to push it away, but would she consider New Orleans? Shaking his head, he wisely decided not to broach the subject. They'd talked long into the night about her ex's attitudes toward her commitment to work, which Cash didn't share. In fact, they'd wound up talking shop, trading information about choosing commercial properties and attracting customers. The bar and fitness businesses were different, but there were plenty of similarities, too. Both of them loved being their own boss.

Turning toward her, he huskily said, "You're really getting to me, Marley." She was more like him than any other woman he'd known, and he liked her just the way she was—willful and headstrong. And sexy as hell.

She sent him a lopsided smile, then said, "Let's hurry. It's freezing out here."

He'd rather have stayed in bed where it was warmer. Her eyes said she felt the same way. He glanced across the avenue at a gay bar called the Duplex before his eyes settled on white statues of human figures in a triangular park that Marley had said was called Sheridan Square. "Which way now?"

"Straight down Christopher Street."

Since her parents lived in the same block as Big

Apple Brides, Cash could barely believe he'd managed to avoid meeting them while dating Edie. Following Marley's lead, he fell silent as they turned down Christopher, taking in boutiques that catered to the unconventional: one sported chains and leather masks, another offered palm and tarot readings, and yet another, apartment renovation based on the principles of feng shui.

To his right, the scent of coffee beans spilled onto the street, more deliciously pungent than anything Cash had ever smelled. With Marley beside him, the city seemed to lack any trace of Cash's more foreboding initial impressions. "I hated it when I first came here," he admitted.

"Out-of-towners say it can be overwhelming."

Horns were blaring, taxis were zipping around each other jockeying for position, and the sidewalks were teeming with people. When they rounded the corner onto Hudson Street, he said, "Well, it sounds like I'm about to get a dose of southern charm right here in the city."

She laughed. "Granny Ginny definitely provides that."

"She sounds like a character."

"She is." Marley sighed. "I'm just glad to have the morning off. Until we got shot at, I didn't realize how scared I was at the Dardens'. Edie mentioned her meeting with Pete Shriver the other night, but she downplayed the danger. If I'd known about the security issues earlier, I don't know that I would have taken the job. Now…well, it's been bothering me more than I've wanted to admit."

"Which is why you ran after a guy who had a rifle?"

She shrugged. "I acted on impulse."

"Fast reflexes," he commented.

"I act first," she admitted. "Ask questions later. Edie's just the opposite."

"You complement each other."

She looked pleased. "I guess we do."

After a moment, he said, "You could quit."

"It's a great job," she countered. "I've gotten back on my feet financially by working with the Dardens, but I'm glad Pete's saying Julia and I have to exercise inside until this guy's caught." She shrugged. "Anyway, the day off is overdue. I feel like I can get my bearings and relax."

He'd gotten the impression that Marley hadn't rested since her ex left. In her apartment, he'd seen her lists of clients and strategy plans for rebuilding the business. "Maybe not," he suddenly said.

"Uh-oh," she muttered, following Cash's gaze and looking farther down Hudson Street. A *Rate the Dates* van was driving alongside them, and Vinny, their videographer, was leaning from a passenger window, taping them. She shook her head, nodding in the direction of bystanders who were starting to stare. "I feel like a celebrity."

"You are," Cash said. "Kind of."

"Until tonight when our television careers are over."

"They're not supposed to tape until noon. That's the deal," Cash muttered, realizing that hell would break loose if Vinny realized Marley wasn't Edie, something that was becoming more likely as they approached Big Apple Brides. Cash glanced toward the sign, which had come into the line of his vision.

Their videographer had been operating against

all the show's rules, showing up at inopportune times, including at the door of the Four Seasons for the past two mornings where he'd taped Cash and Marley leaving the hotel. Fortunately, police training had made Cash an excellent defensive driver, and on the first morning, he'd managed to lose the van before he and Marley reached Brooklyn, which meant Vinny hadn't found out that Marley was impersonating her sister. This morning, Cash had lost the man, as well, when he'd taken Marley home to change for breakfast.

"Great," said Marley nervously, reading his thoughts.

Cash lifted his voice, shouting at Vinny, keeping his tone amiable. "You're not supposed to tape us until we go to the studio."

"It'll only work in your favor," Vinny yelled back from the van, the tape still rolling. "The audience will think you're really crazy about each other. Everybody knows you're going to win."

"We hope," Cash called. "But we're going to complain when we get to the studio. We deserve our privacy."

The motor revved and the van surged into traffic, speeding away. Marley's voice caught. "It does look like we might win."

"I hope," Cash said. "Don't you?" When she hesitated, he guessed, "The curse?"

"The Bennings have been on a losing streak when it comes to dating."

"Not you."

She merely rolled her eyes. "I got divorced."

"No other dates in college?"

"Subconsciously," she said, "I think I was too afraid to try. You know, with Granny Ginny always scaring the daylights out of me where men were concerned. Besides, Chris got interested in me pretty early on."

"So, how can you call yourself unlucky? The divorce rate's fifty percent."

She considered a moment as if to say he might have a point. And Vinny's candid footage had left the impression that Cash and Marley couldn't wait for *Rate the Dates* to end—and their real romance to begin.

Not so, the other couples. The contestants from New Jersey had begun to fight over the man's ex-girlfriend, and as much as Cash hated to stereotype, the people from Connecticut were dyed-in-the-wool WASPs. While they shared similar interests—sailing, antiquing and playing tennis—they weren't exactly setting the world on fire like him and Marley.

Cash captured her lips again, the heat of the kiss coming as no surprise, the skin of her cheek cool and smooth, warming against his. They rubbed noses, then kept walking with their heads together, their foreheads almost touching while the wind sweeping down from South Ferry blew snow into their hair.

"I think you're going to like them," Marley suddenly said.

He hadn't known she was so worried, and he'd hoped there wouldn't be any tension between himself and Edie, although he doubted it. The sisters— all the family members, in fact—seemed to keep in contact via their cell phones, and within a day, Marley had assured him that Edie had no hurt feelings.

"Your parents seemed nice on the phone," he said. "Your whole family's nice." Everyone had pitched in to help Edie start her business, and the same had been true when Marley opened Fancy Abs. Despite the usual familial fights and tensions, everyone ate together at least once a week. Viv Benning insisted on it.

Marley's eyes turned soulful. "We are."

When she'd told him about her marriage, he'd read between the lines. She'd hoped she and Chris would wind up with the same happily-ever-after enjoyed by Joe and Viv. Cash's chest felt suddenly tight, and he found himself missing the only family he'd known, which was lost now. "Close families take work."

"And there are always skeletons."

He sure had a bunch of them. "So true."

She chuckled, now pointing at a brick building with a green awning. "That's where I grew up." She paused. "And where we were the first time I remember meeting Granny Ginny. Edie and I were three when we left Florida, and while you'd think I'd remember her from that time, I don't. She came to visit us one Christmas, though, when we were four or five. And I remember her showing us pictures of the old plantation in Florida where we'd been born. It made a big impression. Jasper Hartley, Mom's first husband, our biological dad—had always lived on the plantation, and after Mom finished college, she and Jasper moved in with his mother. The place is huge. Mom claims they hardly ever even saw Granny. Granny Ginny helped Mom care for us when we were babies. And then Jasper died."

"You call him Jasper?"

She nodded. "I didn't even know him. And Joe's always been my pop."

"Edie said Jasper was a character, just like his mother."

"She wasn't lying," assured Marley, her eyes twinkling in a way that did crazy things to his heart. "Granny Ginny's as cute as a button. And Jasper was really handsome, but hard-drinking and given to chain-smoking cigars."

"Ah. A bad boy," said Cash.

Marley laughed. "You know the type?"

"Intimately," he drawled. "Being born that way myself."

She shook her head. "Bad boys," she repeated. "When it comes to them, we Benning females have a weakness."

His mouth twisted into a wry smile. "Hmm. Why am I not more upset about that, Marley?"

With the words, they'd reached a gold revolving door, and as Marley pushed through it, she sent a dark glance over her shoulder. "I really don't know," she said, right before the door spit them both into a well-appointed lobby. "Because you should be upset."

He followed her toward the elevators. "Why?"

"Because it was that weakness for bad boys that led to the curse, which in turn, will affect your romance with me."

"You don't really believe in the curse, do you?" he asked as the elevator doors shut and they began to ascend.

Rather than answering directly, Marley hardened the expression of her face, her brows furrowing and her lips collapsing into a resigned line. "You're about to meet Granny," she finally returned, blowing out a shaky breath as if to brace herself. "So, I'll just let you judge for yourself."

8

A HALF HOUR LATER, Marley was seated at the dining table, next to Cash, who was digging into a plate piled with Marley's mother's hash browns, ham and her version of eggs Benedict, which the family called eggs Benning. Plucking a warm roll from another basket her mother had just brought from the kitchen, Marley tore off a corner and tried to ignore Cash's equally warm hand, which was under the table and gliding along her leg, hidden by a lace tablecloth.

Leaning close, so only she could hear, he whispered, "Too bad you're not wearing a dress."

Scandalous, she thought, sending him a smile. Inhaling scents of the yeasty bread, she leaned, took another sip of coffee and enjoyed the sensations rippling through her as Cash's fingers curled on her thigh. Since her divorce, Marley had definitely missed sex. Cash squeezed for a delicious moment before his palm traveled upward, resetting near the leg band of her underwear. Buttery heat that put the rolls to shame wafted through her limbs, rising like smoke from an oven, and while she knew she should tell him to stop, she couldn't bring herself to do so. Not that she could get a word in edgewise.

Granny Ginny had taken center stage throughout

the meal as she always did. And as usual, the bird-like woman was dressed to the nines, wearing a pink suit with old-fashioned square buttons that matched a pink fur-collared coat and pillbox hat hanging from the coat rack near the door. Her pearl-handled cane rested against the side of the dining table, and plain bobby pins held back yellow-blond ringlets curling on her temples, a stark contrast to the piercing blue eyes that seemed to leap from pale, papery skin.

Compared to Joe's laid-back plaid flannel shirt, jeans and Mets cap that covered his balding hair, or their mother's denim dress over which she still wore an apron, Granny's outfit looked almost formal. Bridget, of course, had inherited Granny Ginny's shopping genes, and she was clad in a faux-leather micromini, tight long-sleeved midriff top, fish-net stockings and combat boots; a tawny pug dog whom she'd named Mug curled at her feet. Edie was seated next to Bridget, wearing a simple gray dress. Despite Granny Ginny's entertaining rendition of family stories, Edie seemed distracted, probably worrying over the security issues involved with Julia Darden's wedding.

Marley wasn't sure how she felt about Granny Ginny grabbing all the attention. In part, she was glad, and judging from Cash's relieved expression, he shared the feeling. In his fancy trousers, he'd looked very cute, but also overly dressed, at least for him, and while he'd been trying to hide his long-suffering guy-meeting-parents look, Marley could tell he'd been bracing himself for all contingencies.

Without Granny present, they would have spent the meal talking about the stars they'd met at the movie premiere and her and Cash's chance of winning the grand prize tonight on *Rate the Dates*. Just thinking about it, excitement coursed through Marley, even if she couldn't ignore the nagging feeling that something would go wrong. Still, after tonight, maybe she could get her life dreams back on track and open her own health spa again. And then...

The Four Seasons. A shiver claimed her shoulders as she looked at Cash. No doubt, she'd be back in bed with him tonight, after the show. He returned her gaze, his eyes hot on hers, full of intent, and they stayed that way until Granny's voice redirected their attention.

"That ring!" she exclaimed, and when Marley turned, it was to see Granny raise a limp-wristed, lily-pale hand that was trembling like a leaf. In a southern accent so heavy it was almost indecipherable to Marley, and far thicker than Cash's, Granny drawled, "Lawdy, Miss Bridget, where on earth did you get that? And why didn't I notice it before this very minute?"

"I designed it for Julia Darden, but she chose another one." Holding out her hand and splaying fingers with black-painted nails, Bridget admired her own handiwork, a bursting cluster of sparkling cubic zirconia. "*I* liked it," she said, sounding miffed.

Granny Ginny only shuddered, causing Marley to shoot Cash a warning glance, so he'd know to expect some strange turn in the conversation. "That ring," Granny repeated. "I...my, oh, my, I do think I might swoon...." Quickly reaching, she grasped the stem of a water glass and took a sip as if to revive herself. "You say you designed it, Miss Bridget? Why, that's impossible!"

Marley couldn't help but smile, since Granny always prefaced their names with the word Miss. She watched as Bridget's lips parted. Her youngest sister looked faintly guilty as if she'd just been accused of stealing. "No, it's not impossible," Bridget countered. "I saw the image of this ring in a dream."

Granny gasped. "A dream?" When Bridget nodded, Granny exclaimed, "Why, that's mighty mysterious! No doubt, the ghost of Lavinia Delroy has a hand in this."

"Lavinia Delroy?" gasped Bridget. "That would make perfect sense! I just thought my own subconscious mind was working in my sleep. I mean, a lot of creative people claim they get new ideas that way, but..."

"Lavinia Delroy is long gone," Viv put in flatly. "And she certainly isn't planting ideas for jewelry designs in my daughter's head!"

Pointedly ignoring everyone but Bridget, Granny Ginny leaned forward and said, "You swear you've never seen anything like that ring before?"

Her blue eyes wide, Bridget shook her head in confusion, and glanced again at the ring that she'd hoped Julia Darden would wear to signify her engagement, along with a simple gold band.

Spots of color were slowly returning to Granny's otherwise chalk-white cheeks. "Oh, it really is a good thing that I've come to visit," she announced ominously. Inhaling deeply, she plunged on. "Miss Bridget, you've designed a ring," she claimed, "that's an exact replica of the long-lost Hartley diamond. It was worn by the ghost bride of Hartley House and disappeared over a hundred years ago. I should know," she said reasonably, "because it's believed to be hidden somewhere in my house." Hunkering her shoulders, Granny looked slowly around the table before saying, "And that could mean only one thing."

Even Marley felt her heart skip a beat at the dramatic tone, and she glanced at Cash, who looked as drawn in by the story as the rest of the family. "What Granny?" Marley couldn't help but ask.

"That absolutely none of the recent events are my imagination, and Jasper's ghost really has come back to haunt the plantation with renewed verve."

Casting another quick glance at Cash, Marley could see hints of doubt in his eyes, and she didn't blame him for feeling confused. Granny Ginny never told a story linearly, but rather circled her topics, slowly drawing listeners in, forcing them to put her narrative together, piece by piece, like a puzzle. Now looking completely overwhelmed, Granny glanced slowly around the room once more, as if she simply didn't know where to begin, and then she clucked her tongue and said, "But of course you girls have probably forgotten all about Forrest Hartley, Miss Marissa and Reverend George, and how the wedding curse came to be."

"How could they forget?" Viv said dryly. "You remind them every time you visit."

Granny pierced her with a gaze. "Exactly. And I haven't visited since last year, which means they've surely forgotten."

Marley's mother heaved a loud sigh. She'd always been disturbed by the idea of her first husband's ghost haunting the old Florida plantation Ginny called home, which was probably understandable.

Marley, however, was actually starting to enjoy herself, glad for the reprieve. She'd been so worried about her appearance on *Rate the Dates,* and whether she and Cash would win, not to mention worried for Edie, since Julia's stalker—if that's what he really was—could jeopardize the wedding. And then there was the fact that Marley was sleeping with Cash Champagne.... With so much on her plate, she could definitely use a distraction, and Granny Ginny certainly provided that, even if the fact of the curse had given Marley pause since her divorce.

"You can't believe the ring on Bridget's finger is an exact replica of the Hartley diamond," Viv was arguing. "Now, Ginny, you know that everything you're saying is pure nonsense. You've filled the girls' minds with these stories for so long that you've convinced them they're cursed when it comes to romance. It's just not healthy."

"You've seen Miss Marissa's portrait hanging in the parlor of the plantation, Viv," Granny Ginny countered pragmatically. "And that means you've seen the ring."

Viv squared her shoulders. "I remember no such thing," she assured. "If I'd ever seen a picture of a diamond that was exactly like the ring on Bridget's finger, I'd have remembered."

"Apparently not," said Ginny with a sniff.

Viv tried once more. "We have a guest today. And so many other things to talk about, so I won't have you filling my girls' minds with these stories."

But nobody heard. They were staring at Granny expectantly, even Joe, so the only concession Granny made to Viv's protests was to stare at Cash sympathetically and intone in a soft drawl, "Son, I'm glad you've come today. You might as well know what you've gotten yourself into before you find out the hard way."

Before Cash could respond, Bridget cut in. "Now, you're sure the ring I'm wearing looks exactly like the Hartley diamond? The one worn by Miss Marissa, the ghost bride? And we can prove it, since the picture's hanging in your parlor?"

"Absolutely," assured Ginny.

Bridget inhaled sharply, her gaze shooting to her finger once more. "Basically, that proves that the ghosts at Hartley House exist, right? I mean, Miss Marissa's portrait was painted years ago, long before I had the dream in which I first saw this ring, and so if she's really wearing it in the picture..."

"She's not," Viv assured.

"Maybe you're wrong, Mom," protested Bridget. "All we have to do is go look, and if I could find the ring, maybe it would put the spirits in Hartley House to rest."

Taking a deep breath, Marley glanced around the room in which she'd spent so much time growing up, her heart swelling as she took in all the familiar items: a mantle decorated with family snapshots, bookshelves crammed with well-read paperbacks, walls adorned with art she and her sisters had made when they were kids.

And then she looked at Bridget again. Looking intrigued, her sister reached for a bagel, smeared it liberally with lox spread, ripped off a piece, then held it under the table, rolling her eyes when she saw their mother's look of warning. "Mom, Pug-Mug has to eat," Bridget cooed defensively before turning her attention to Ginny again. "You're telling the truth, Granny?"

"Oh, precious, would I tell a lie?" Granny Ginny asked innocently, although Marley—as well as everyone else at the table, Marley suspected—had decided Ginny Hartley was no stranger to the fine art of splitting hairs. Not that the observation made the curse any less real, though, judging by the Benning sisters' uncanny failures in love.

After another quick glance at Cash, whose hands were still doing wonderfully arousing things under the table, Marley took in the ring that Bridget wore on her right ring finger. It really was striking, a glittering tangle of cubic zirconia.

"How long are you going to keep us in suspense?" Joe asked.

Granny smiled. "Oh, another moment or two."

Joe chuckled. He'd encouraged their mom's contact with this lonely relative, and he enjoyed her immensely.

Now Granny sighed deeply. "I suppose I need to start at the very beginning for Mr. Champagne, even if you all have heard my tale before." She sent Cash a long look, then said, "You see...years ago, my ancestor, confederate officer Forrest Hartley, was struck down in his prime."

Everyone urged her on, saying, "Yes?"

Only Viv uttered a sigh of helpless exasperation. She said, "Girls, not a word of this is true."

But Granny continued. "It was Forrest's daddy who built Hartley House, which is haunted, and where I've spent my declining years." She raised a hand. "Mind you, I'll get to the ghosts, but first you have to understand..." She paused, as if unsure where to begin. "Forrest and Miss Marissa—I'm talking about Miss Marissa Jennings," she clarified, "whose people came from Macon. Well, these two were madly in love and about to marry. Forrest was in town with the rebel forces, of course—he was a confederate soldier—but he was to return to Hartley House before heading for the war front, so he and Miss Marissa could be wed by Reverend George. This was to occur at midnight, in the south parlor, under the grand chandelier that hangs there until this day, along with the picture of Miss Marissa, where she's wearing the original ring that matches the one Bridget's got on."

"Hmm. Reverend George?" prompted Joe.

"I'll get to him, too," Granny Ginny promised, taking a moment to sip her water. "So..." she began again. "As I was saying, it was nearly midnight. Now, this was the height of the war, remember, so from not too far off, you could hear cannons, bugles and trumpets, as well as the hack-hack sound of men clearing a path through the woods with machetes."

She leaned forward, staring at each listener in turn. "Only Miss Marissa was in the house. Her own family had already fled to relatives in Georgia—" Lifting a hand, she wagged a finger in caution, then hunkered down lower, her dark blue eyes flashing with intrigue, but their expression far off, too, as if she were imagining the twisted roots of moss-hung cypress trees stretching deep into the loamy soil of moonlit swamps near the house. "Fleeing to Georgia," she repeated. "A bad move, given what those damn Yankees did to Atlanta."

While Granny heaved a deep sigh, as if getting her bearings, Marley swallowed hard. She'd always felt safe from war, but given Granny Ginny's pungent language, the idea of it seemed much more real. She could almost see fire as bullets flew through the night, and booms of smoke following in the wake of cannonballs. It seemed so real that she was suddenly absolutely sure there was a curse, and feeling a sharp pain twist in her chest, she cast a quick glance at Cash. Was whatever was happening between them really doomed to fail?

Looking chagrined, Granny abruptly added, "Well, Marissa was alone in the house, *almost.* Lavinia was there, of course. She was a Creole housekeeper," she continued, now speaking to Cash. "A tiny firecracker of a woman who'd come up from island country, through New Orleans, with bright dark eyes and skin the shiny, toasted red of glazed clay pottery."

Granny Ginny's voice dropped. "Nobody in Big Swamp, Florida—that's the name of our town— dared to speak of it, but even back then, it was well known that housekeeping wasn't Lavinia's only trade. She had a sideline business selling herbs and making voodoo dolls, and in that part of the South, during the war, with so much evil afoot…well, let's just say, her business was booming. One pin," assured Granny Ginny, lifting a shaky, arthritic finger and stabbing the air, "And your victim was a goner."

"Really?"

Cash's voice drew Marley from her reverie. Somehow, his obvious skepticism was comforting. Even though she'd become convinced she was cursed since the divorce, the idea occasionally hit her full force. It seemed so real. And so terrible. What if she never found love again? "What?" she teased in a soft whisper, pushing away her thoughts. "Do you have victims in mind?"

"A few," he whispered back, so only she could hear. "You?" Another firm squeeze of his hand on her thigh indicated that if she were looking to pierce her enemies with a pin, he hoped he wasn't one of them.

She thought of her ex-husband, then said as he had, "A few."

"Oh, yes," Granny Ginny was assuring. "One pin could fell a man like a tree, but that's a story for another day. Right now, what you should remember is that Lavinia had prophetic dreams, so perhaps she could plant ideas in people's minds. Now, before I say anything more about Lavinia, I'd better mention Reverend George, who refused to run." As she shook her head, thinking back to that time in history, blond curls bounced around her face. "The South was his home," she declared, her voice filled with pride. And then she added, "He was a real man."

Cash and Joe raised eyebrows. "A real man?"

Her quick nod held significance. "Oh, yes. Reverend George held his ground against all the forces of evil." Sounding scandalized, she added, "He even gave solace to dying Yankees, or so it was rumored. He was a man of God, first. Not partial to party politics, so you can see why Miss Marissa and Forrest wanted him to officiate over their wedding ceremony.

"It was Reverend George for whom Miss Marissa was waiting when she first heard hooves thundering, the sound coming suddenly, like bats from hell out of the night, flying down the shell-covered red dirt road, while Yankees in the woods used machetes to approach, beating back thickets and brambles."

Leaning farther forward, Granny Ginny lowered her voice another notch. "As the Union advanced, Miss Marissa realized she'd waited too long for love, and too long to leave Hartley House. Reverend George, it would later turn out, had been waylaid at rifle-point. As much as he wanted to get to Hartley House and marry the couple, he was tending the wounded. And Forrest..."

Granny Ginny shrugged. "Well, I'll get to him in a minute. Knowing she and Lavinia were doomed, Marissa prayed her beau wouldn't try to leave the safety of the rebel forces and come for her. If he did, he'd surely be killed by Yankees.

"Lavinia, of course, had survived plenty of wars before this, so she wasn't about to lay down and die for any northern soldiers. In addition to selling spices, herbs and making dolls, I should mention again that she was said to have premonitions, prophetic dreams and such.

"It was probably due to this that Lavinia had already thought to hide all the family jewelry in the ceiling of a root cellar, except the ring that Miss Marissa wore...." Granny Ginny pierced the audience with her eyes again before zeroing in on the ring on Bridget's finger. "Miss Marissa, so in love, refused to take off that ring...the priceless cluster of diamonds that vanished on that fateful night...the ring that, once found, will remove the curse hanging over the heads of you girls...."

"But where is it?" exclaimed Bridget.

"Fate must be drawing us close to finding it, Miss Bridget," Granny assured, "since you've designed a replica."

"I hope so," Edie said, speaking for the first time.

Granny Ginny plunged on. "Needless to say, the Yankees entered the house. They stripped it to its skeleton, taking everything except the parlor chandelier. Why it remained is a mystery. It was made of heavy silver, though, and its hooks were in the ceiling so deep that, rumor has it, the Yankees just gave up. 'Sides, they were more interested in using gators from the swamps for target practice and exploring Forrest Hartley's well-stocked liquor cabinets."

She paused, letting that sink in. "Not that the Yankees didn't want that chandelier, mind you. It was a real beaut. Why, they tugged, and they pulled, but just like the ghosts that haunt the parlor in which it still hangs, the chandelier belonged to Hartley House." Her voice turned darkly ominous. "And it wasn't leaving."

"What happened to Marissa?" Marley couldn't help but prompt, her heart skipping a beat when she sent Cash another glance. Unfortunately, he was starting to look pensive. Not a good sign. Maybe he was starting to believe all this....

"Well...Lavinia and Miss Marissa fled to the swamp and hid," Granny Ginny said, "which is why Miss Marissa was struck down."

"Struck down?" they all echoed, even though they'd heard the story countless times.

Granny Ginny nodded. "It was from that vantage point, hidden in the murky water with gators circling her and the wide skirt of her wedding gown ballooning, that Miss Marissa saw her lover slain, cut down in his prime by the sword of a Yankee. By then, she'd lost Lavinia, who's thought to have floated away in the current."

"Where was Forrest?" Marley couldn't help but ask.

"Forrest was on foot, and a union soldier was on horseback, riding fast down the shell-road in the dark of midnight, which was lit only by stars and a full moon. Forrest was doing everything he could to come home to Hartley House. He wanted only to see his beloved, and to live until Reverend George married them. He was close, too. Almost to the house, and he didn't see the enemy soldier behind him. The man leaned down as he rode, the night air rent by the sound of a sword drawn from his sheath. It rose high, glinting, arching as he bore down on poor Forrest, whose only thought was for his bride, and…"

She took a deep breath. "If I give any more detail, I'll swoon," she apologized although her eyes were bright with relish as she spoke. "No neighbors helped, mind you. The ancestors of Mavis Benchley, who lives on the adjacent plantation to this day, were of no more use than they are in present times. They were hiding in a root cellar the Yankees didn't find."

She shook her head. "No, sir, the Benchleys would never lift a finger to help a Hartley, sad but true. How the Benchleys live with themselves, I'll never know. That's why, around Hartley house, after the war, we came to have an expression for all those who do wrong. "Lower than a Benchley," she intoned, her tone brooking no argument.

"So, while the Benchleys lay safe and sound in their root cellar right next door, a flash of light appeared in the sky. It was a cannonball aimed toward the swamp. Now, don't forget, Miss Marissa had just witnessed her lover slain, so some thought she died of a broken heart, and others say it was the cannonball that cut her down. Maybe even just a stray bullet. The real facts about her death remain a mystery. Whatever the case, she uttered a curse on Hartley House in a fit of pique, saying that until she was reunited with her lover, those associated with Hartley House would never find romance. Which is why Forrest's descendants are cursed in love to this very day. Some say she died wearing Forrest's ring. But Lavinia has come to many Hartley women in dreams—and that would mean Bennings, too, of course—and she's said that Marissa hid the ring in the house."

"But why would finding the ring end the curse?" asked Bridget, confused.

This definitely added a new spin to the tales Marley had already heard. "Yeah," she said. "I don't get it."

Granny stared at her a moment. "And I thought it was obvious!" she exclaimed. "Without the ring, there can be no wedding, so it must be found before Marissa and Forrest can reunite."

Viv groaned. "That's ridiculous."

"It doesn't completely make sense. I mean, if Marissa hid the ring," Joe offered. "And she and Forrest are ghosts, then why doesn't she just tell him where she put it?"

"And then they can have a ghost-wedding," Marley said, pleased to hear her own peal of laughter, since her father was right and this did sound far-fetched.

Granny wasn't put off by the skepticism, though. "If there's one thing I can tell you about ghosts," she assured, "It's that nothing they do makes sense by the standards of the living."

"The curse wasn't very nice," Marley couldn't help but say.

"Marissa was spoiled," Granny admitted. "Only sixteen and overly used to party dresses, new ponies and dances."

Ever the cop, Cash asked, "They never found her body?"

Granny Ginny rolled her eyes as if to say Cash was being too technical and not hearing her story in the right spirit. "These were Yankees," she declared, as if Cash, of all people, should understand. "No one could survive the horrifying assault, and who was left to look for a body?"

"Good point," Cash conceded.

"Any record of Lavinia was lost, as well," Granny Ginny continued sadly. "And today the only evidence of her is the way she still bustles around Hartley House, just as scrawny and bossy as ever."

Bridget sounded breathless. "You've really seen these ghosts, Granny Ginny? You swear you're not making all this up?"

Granny Ginny puffed her cheeks and sighed as she blew out a long, deflating breath, suddenly looking even older and very tired. "I see them every night of my life," she assured. "And lately—" her blue eyes narrowed "—things round Hartley House have gotten worse. Far worse. Yes, it's mighty peculiar. The ghost are destroying my sleep. Especially that fool woman, Lavinia Delroy.

"Why, that woman won't shut her trap." Granny Ginny leaned back and mocked her, "'Now, Ginny,' she says to me, 'you're getting on in years, and you ought to make up with Mavis Benchley before you die. And put this house in order. Find the missing wedding ring and end the curse because those Benning girls are of marriageable age now. If you don't find a way to put those ghosts to rest, Marley will never win on *Rate the Dates*. And Edie and Bridget don't have a prayer. Pay your taxes, too.'"

Granny Ginny looked furious now. "Marissa is no better," she declared. "Pacing to and fro in that bloody wedding gown that smells of the swamp with a cannonball in her hand. And the ghost groom? Well...he isn't nearly as good-looking as in his daguerreotype pictures, being headless now, but I forgive him. After all, he's my kin."

She paused thoughtfully. "Same with Jasper, my son," she continued. "Every night, I smell his cigars and whiskey, and hear the tread of his boots on the wooden floors. He tracks in mud, just the same as when he was a boy. So there you have it," she finished. "That's why you girls are old maids."

"They're not old maids!" Viv exclaimed. "Girls don't marry young anymore."

Granny didn't look convinced. "Maybe not," she said, but it was clear she was only being polite.

As she had many times, Marley tried to take it all in—a love affair torn asunder, a bride and groom who walked the halls of a plantation at night, and a lost wedding ring. Cash tilted his head downward and shot her a long look, peering at her under heavy eyelids, as if to assure her that all this was a crock.

"The haunting's gotten worse," Granny continued quickly. "Probably due to the girls' marriageable age. I don't mix well with Yankees," she admitted to no one in particular, "but I strongly felt it my duty to come north again. And then, when I saw Marley, trying to get herself married off on TV—"

Marley's jaw dropped. "I was not—"

"While you're here, I'm going to go down to the plantation, Granny," Bridget cut in. "Would you let me? I want to look for the ring. Maybe I can find it, and…"

End the curse.

Suddenly, Marley just couldn't take the conversation anymore. It seemed too real. What if it really was true? What if she never found love? Had Chris been her only chance, one lost because of her family history? She sighed. Her mother was right. Granny had filled her mind with these stories, and it really wasn't healthy. Murmuring a quick "Excuse me," she placed her napkin beside her plate and headed for the living room, just so she could clear her head.

From behind her, she could still hear her grandmother's voice. She was addressing Bridget. "Oh, you used to love that old chandelier in the parlor," she was saying. "I'd tell Marley and Edie that, when they were older, they could take down the prisms and play dress-up with them. Use them for earrings. When you were an itty-bitty baby, the only place you'd sleep was on an old round pedestal table, right beneath that chandelier, in the parlor. Tucked into your basinet, of course. You'd stare up at those prisms for hours as if you were starstruck. It was as if you realized that chandelier was just about the only thing the Yankees left during the war."

As Marley reached the living room, her nose suddenly wiggled and she wondered if something was burning in the kitchen. But no, for the briefest moment, she could swear she smelled... "A cigar," she suddenly whispered, spinning around—only to find herself facing Cash.

"You okay?"

She shook her head. "I don't know. Do you smell something?"

His eyes found hers and he squinted, looking unsettled and incredibly sexy. With his nose scrunched, she could see the boy he'd been. For a second, he looked truly surprised, almost as if he, too, had caught a whiff of cigars and whiskey and believed in magic. "No," he returned flatly, shaking his head, the world-weary expression returning to his eyes.

"My father, Jasper, smoked cigars," she said. But she hadn't smelled them, of course. Granny Ginny was such a remarkable storyteller that Marley had simply gotten sucked into the tale. So had Cash, and he was a die-hard cynic. Shaking her mind to clear it of confusion, Marley glanced at her watch and gasped. "We have to leave soon," she said, "to make the studio."

"I almost forgot about the show," Cash admitted.

"Easy when you listen to her talk, isn't it?"

He nodded, his lips curling into a smile. "Your Granny Ginny's really something."

"I wish you'd been able to talk to my parents more."

He hesitated, then locked gazes with hers and said, "Another time."

Her heart fluttered. Cash Champagne meant to come back. She took a deep breath. Surely, Granny was wrong. Let Bridget and Edie believe in these tall tales. She'd risked loving once with Chris, and Cash was right. The divorce rate really was fifty percent. What had happened to her wasn't even unusual. She wasn't the only divorcée who'd felt heartbreak, either. Most of them had.

"We're going to win," she whispered, determined to block out Granny Ginny's discouraging omens.

"Damn straight," said Cash. As he smiled back, she had the fleeting, unbidden thought that they might remember this day in the future. In a flash fantasy, she imagined telling their kids about how they'd proved a wedding curse wrong.

Once more, she shook her head to clear it of confusion. She was having sex with Cash, she reminded herself, not marrying him. If there was any doubt about that, his heavy, warm hand was circling her back, stroking her slowly and with such intent that she had to fight back shudders. He was soliciting hormones, not the words *until death do we part.*

Nevertheless, what if some part of this story was true? Marley wondered as she always did, no matter how hard she tried to push aside the thoughts. Maybe the Bennings' lives were touched by a paranormal element. What was the likelihood of Edie being hired to plan a celebrity wedding, after all? Or for Marley, who led such an average life, to be railroaded onto a national television show with a man who'd been her own sister's sort-of boyfriend? Or to meet him on the exact same day that marked her divorce from Chris? Or, and this was more important, to feel as if she could fall in love with somebody new, just weeks after she'd sworn off sex forever? And then there was the fact that they really might win tonight on *Rate the Dates.*

Of course, those were all good things....

She glanced at Cash, only to find him still looking at her, his eyes hot and dark. Even if they hated each other, which they didn't, they wouldn't be able to keep their hands off each other, so, maybe his meeting Granny Ginny was just one more piece in a twist of fate that seemed racing to some conclusion....

"C'mon," he murmured softly. "You didn't let her get to you, did you?" He sighed, lifting a finger and trailing it down her cheek. "There are a million holes in her story, Marley. How could Marissa see her lover on the road when she was in the swamp?" he challenged. "And why did the union soldiers leave a chandelier when they were looting?" His eyes grew steamy, glistening and warm as they flicked over her. "After the way we made love last night, do you really think your romantic life is doomed?"

"Spoken like an ex-cop."

Leaning, he pressed his lips firmly to hers. The kiss ignited. Flames burst inside her. At the touch of his mouth, every thought flew from her mind and only dark sensation seemed to matter. When he drew back, he said, "Women suffering from wedding curses don't kiss like that."

"Sex isn't the problem," she countered. "It's romance."

He smiled. "I thought that kiss was romantic."

She almost smiled back. "It was."

He pressed his forehead to hers. "We're going to win that show tonight, Marley Benning," he promised. "In just a few hours, you're going to have the money to reopen your business, and your whole life's going to be smooth sailing, from here on out."

She laughed. "You're sure of this?"

"Yeah. I'm with your mom on this. There's no curse."

"You really think we're going to get lucky tonight?"

At that, he just laughed. "One way or another," he said. "Oh, yeah."

9

MARLEY TRIED TO FORCE HERSELF to relax in the studio chair next to Cash, but her pulse was ticking wildly and her belly was jittery. Knowing her parents, sisters and Granny Ginny were watching, she somehow managed to send a fleeting smile toward the camera. Cash twined his fingers through hers, clearly not caring that her palms were clammy. When she squeezed, he tightened his fingers, squeezing back, making her heart miss a beat and making her hope Granny Ginny was wrong. If they won, wouldn't that prove there wasn't a curse?

"We're doing good," Cash whispered.

"Yeah." She sent him a quick smile, realizing that as much as she wanted the grand prize, winning also meant she could share this excitement with Cash.

The mood of the studio audience was hard to discern. She squinted, trying to see them, but the stage was flooded with lights that hurt her eyes. Beyond the cameras, she could barely make out rows of seats; everything beyond the stage was pitch dark. Only the noise gave away the presence of a crowd. Whenever the audience was asked to vote by using the scoring pad built in to their armrests, applause and gasps sounded.

Trevor Milane was seated next to the corn-fed blond cohost. Now Trevor was saying, "You've had all week to think about these couples. You've seen their every move…how they kiss, hug, talk to each other.

"All along, you've been mentally tallying your impressions. You know who's hot and who's not. Who's in it for the romance, and who's just angling to get into the sack. Tonight, it's your turn to take center stage. Only you can guess: Will anybody here make it to the altar? Which is the most likely couple?"

"Cash and Edie!" somebody yelled.

"The jury's still out," called Trevor. "Are you ready to cast your vote on another steamy date?"

The crowd went wild. Staring into the darkness, Marley could hear stomping and clapping. Shouting voices melded together, but she heard someone call Edie and Cash's names again.

"We were good," she whispered, leaning away from the microphone pinned to the collar of her navy dress, thinking of the dreamy night at Alexandria's and the fun they'd had at the movie premiere and playing golf.

"Dynamite," he agreed.

She just hoped that dynamite wasn't going to blow up in their faces. She'd been so sure someone might realize she wasn't Edie. Over the past week, however, her luck had changed. And this had been the most incredible day, no matter what Granny Ginny portended. She shook her head to clear it of confusion. On the one hand, she had to admit that she and her sisters hadn't been lucky in love. On the other, she felt wonderful right now. And all the things Cash had told her about himself had checked out, right?

Just one week ago, she'd been spending most of her time alone, making lists of things she could do to get her life back on track. Now, she was moving faster than she'd ever believed possible. With Cash beside her, she felt like she'd been shot out of a cannon. She was headed for something great; she could feel it in her bones. Definitely, Granny Ginny was wrong.

"We're going to show you another segment now," said Trevor. "It will remind you of another dream date you watched this week. These couples have been everywhere from the best restaurants in Manhattan to sports spas. They've modeled diamonds from Cartier's as well as mud-splattered jeans. You've seen 'em fight, and you've seen 'em love. Now, take a good look folks..." Trevor raised his voice. "Roll 'em!"

Cash's hand tightened in hers once more as they shifted their attention to a monitor. Her heart missed a beat as she watched the couple from Connecticut playfully splashing each other in a hot tub. Next, the people from New Jersey were shown. They were fighting about the man's ex-girlfriends, and as Marley watched, she felt encouraged, since the date hardly looked romantic.

"It was your idea to be on this stupid show!" the woman proclaimed as she lifted her glass and tossed champagne into her date's face. Angrily, he ducked beneath the water, then came up, using both hands to slick back his hair. Swiping a hand in the air, he tried to grab her, but she was already running up the stairs of the hot tub, pressing a flattened palm to the top of a skimpy red suit, trying to make sure it stayed on as she fled for the changing room.

"And now," shouted Trevor, "let's look at Edie and Cash."

Beside her, she heard Cash's breath catch. One look and she understood why. She'd never seen anything so sexy in her life. On the monitor, Cash was floating in the Jacuzzi bubbles, his arms wrapping around her back as her legs circled his waist. Holding the champagne glass, he tilted it back, urging her to take a sip. After she did so, he set it aside, leaning closer and kissing her in a way that rivaled great movie kisses. As the kiss grew more intense, her cheeks warmed. They were hugging each other tightly, their mouths moving with yearning. Skin met skin. And somewhere, beyond the cameras, her parents were watching this....

As soon as the tape ended, the audience began casting votes, punching numbers on their armrests, but given what she'd seen, Marley felt confident. "That date was a no-brainer," she mouthed.

"Agreed," whispered Cash.

"All right, folks!" Trevor called. "So far, Cash and Edie are ahead. If they win this date, they may just get that grand prize! After the hot tub date, there's only one left to judge, the movie premiere!"

Marley curled a hand over Cash's biceps, reveling in the heat seeping through the sleeve of his sport coat. As on the first show, he'd worn soft jeans that she knew would feel like butter beneath her hand, as well as a white shirt under the sport coat, which she was fantasizing about removing.... She uttered a shivery breath. In just a few minutes, they were going to win! Granny Ginny would be eating crow, and Marley and Cash would be back at the Four Seasons.

All the studio-audience scores were coming in low, and after this, as Trevor had said, only one date remained. Realizing she was sitting on the edge of her seat, Marley forced herself to sit back. *Try to relax*, she told herself, but she couldn't. Breath whooshed from her when, on a scale of one to ten, the couple from Connecticut received a four. Surprisingly, though, the New Jersey couple got a six.

Trevor laughed. "That fight was spicy! Everybody saw the passion! Now, let's see Cash and Edie!"

Passion? The couple hated each other! Marley's breath was shallow, and when the scores came in, her eyes widened. *A five?* "Only a five for us?" What had gone wrong? Her lips parted, and she glanced at Cash, who looked equally shocked.

"Whoopsy-doopsy for our underdog couple," Trevor said. "Unless they win by three points on the next round, the grand prize might go to our couple from New Jersey. I don't know about you, but I can't wait another minute. Roll the tapes from the movie premiere!"

Marley was in shock. Squaring her shoulders and sitting at full attention, she brought her lips to Cash's ear and whispered, "I can't believe our score."

"It's not over till the fat lady sings," drawled Cash.

But Marley wasn't sure. She watched as the Connecticut couple walked down the red carpet to the movie theater, both dressed to the nines. Both looked as excited as Marley had felt that night, as they gawked at movie stars. Suddenly, the woman almost tripped. As she staggered, trying to regain her balance, her shoe flew off, and she was left standing on the red carpet, sans one high heel.

Turning quickly, her date headed a few paces back, retrieved the shoe and returned. Kneeling, he lifted the shoe gingerly and wiggled it back onto her foot, looking for all the world like Prince Charming.

"Very nice," whispered Marley.

"Stock move," assured Cash under his breath. "I saw a guy do that in Cinderella."

Marley almost laughed. "True. It lacks originality." She sent Cash a grin. He always knew what to say to make her feel better, and he had a great sense of humor. And while he seemed almost rough at times, he wasn't. Face it, she thought. This guy's just about perfect.

"An eight!" Trevor suddenly shouted.

Marley sucked in a breath. The Connecticut couple was behind, but this still wasn't good. Even worse, when the next tape rolled, it showed the New Jersey couple making out in a corner at the premiere, in a way that rivaled Cash and Marley's hot tub kiss. It was as if the movie stars didn't matter to the New Jersey couple in the least.

"Six!" shouted Trevor when the votes were in. "And now for Cash and Edie!"

Marley's heart sank as she watched them on the red-carpeted runway, and her cheeks flushed red with embarrassed heat. She looked okay in the long red dress Miranda had chosen, she thought, but she was gaping at everyone, as if she'd just moved to New York from Kansas. She was a New Yorker, born and bred. She'd seen Willem Dafoe on Broadway one day, and had gotten her hair cut at the same salon as Susan Sarandon, and now she was working out daily with Julia Darden. Nevertheless, there she was, in front of the whole world, craning her neck to stare at everyone from Morgan Freeman to John Travolta to Clint Eastwood. And then she saw him.

Tom Cruise.

She winced as she watched the interplay between herself and Cash. He was urging her forward; she was holding back. It was he who forcibly pulled her to the star and introduced him, and if she were honest, she was glad he'd done so. She was such a fan. She must have seen *Top Gun* a hundred times. She recalled feeling as if she were about to faint as Cash suddenly produced a book he'd bought for the purpose and got her an autograph. Oh, she'd felt ridiculous as he'd taken her from star to star, but it had been so sweet of him....

"Nine!" Trevor suddenly shouted. "It's a nine! The grand prize goes to the underdog couple! Edie and Cash are our winners tonight!"

In a breath, she was on her feet and in Cash's embrace. Tightly wreathing her arms around his neck, Marley had never felt so happy. Silently, she cursed Granny Ginny for filling her with so much doubt. "A curse on the Bennings," she whispered.

"Obviously, your grandmother's wrong," Cash returned, his mouth covering hers, his arms drawing her nearer as he swung her in circles. As her palms registered the strength in his shoulders, the whole front of her felt the heat seeping through his clothes. Bursting inside, she kissed him back. His mouth was moving on hers, his lips turning wet as his tongue found hers, speaking a promise for tonight more convincingly than any words.

The studio audience, the cameras, the bright

lights…all of it vanished when he whispered, "Let's go to bed and celebrate."

SPARKY DARDEN STARED at the television, his heartbeat quickening as he watched the kiss, his gaze flicking over Cash. Sparky had been rooting for the couple, of course, but now…

What was it that niggled him? Shaking his head, Sparky remembered how quickly Cash had moved after he'd heard the gunshot. One minute, he'd been in Sparky's study, where he'd been shooting the breeze. Sparky had stepped out for moment, only to return to see his guest running for the woods, chasing Julia's attacker. Plenty of meetings had followed that event, too, all calculated to bring security up to par. Pete and the police had found shell casings and bullets. With every breath since, Sparky had thanked God for his daughter and Marley's survival.

Not that he trusted the Creator to do him any favors after the way he'd treated people in the hotel business. Still, his daughter was innocent, she'd done nothing wrong, and ever since getting the big C, Sparky had tried to right old wrongs and make amends. Vowing to never again let his daughter sweet-talk him, Sparky studied Cash, thinking of how he'd ingratiated himself on his trips to the estate with Marley. Oh, the man was slick, but in retrospect, Sparky felt it likely that the man had a hidden agenda. He had a distinctive way of moving….

"Damn," he cursed. Where had Cash been when the shots were fired? Had Pete asked? Could Cash have actually fired the shots? Regarding the tire tracks on the highway, maybe they weren't really left by an intruder. Maybe they'd been there earlier, and Cash only claimed he'd seen the man squeal away in an SUV. All week, Sparky had been letting this guy walk right onto his property, but did they know enough about him? Ever since the meetings, Pete had insisted on doing more thorough background checks, but what if it was too late? What if…

"I can't believe this," he whispered.

But hadn't his senses alerted him when he'd first seen Cash on the show? Something about the man had bothered him all week. When *Rate the Dates* cut for a commercial break, Sparky switched to video and hit Play. As he had hundreds of times, he watched the darkly clad figure darting across the lawn, his movements agile. Lithely, the man started up the veranda steps, reaching to his side and unsheathing a knife….

There was no doubt about it. The man who'd attacked him years ago and Cash Champagne were one and the same man.

"WE WON," MARLEY SAID as soon as they were inside the Four Seasons.

Chuckling as she threw her arms around his neck once more, Cash settled his palms on her waist, feeling them warm as they traced the swell of her hips. "Oh, Marley," he said, his voice husky as his tongue stroked the rim of her ear, "did you really think those other couples could beat us?"

Couples. Registering the word, Cash realized he and Marley had become that, and he couldn't help but wonder what was going to happen, whether or not the studio audience would turn out to be right about them staying together. Given how he felt about Marley, he knew that her grandmother couldn't have been more wrong about the curse.

"Just before Trevor announced the winners," she admitted breathlessly, peppering his lips with light smacking kisses, "I was sure the audience had chosen the couple from New Jersey, and deep down, the whole time, I was afraid someone might figure out I wasn't Edie, or that Granny was right."

"She's nuts," Cash assured.

"A good kind of nuts, though," defended Marley. She *had* been fun to be around. "A born storyteller."

And the curse was just that—a story. He, too, had worried about the switch being discovered, but even people from *Celebrity Weddings* hadn't seemed to notice. "If they'd found out you weren't Edie, would that really have proven your grandmother was right and you're jinxed?"

She sighed. "A lot of things do support her theory."

Nodding sagely, Cash leaned back to get a better look at her. Excitement and the night air had made her look positively radiant. She was smiling, her red cheeks bursting with color. Inhaling, he smelled a scent that arrowed straight to his groin, tangling with lust and emotion. "I've got a few theories of my own."

"Such as?"

Rarely at a loss for words, Cash couldn't think. Or maybe he didn't want to. Lowering his head, he kissed her slowly, then he drew away to look into her eyes. "I've got a thousand answers, but I can't think of them right now. There are too many things I want to do besides talk, Marley Benning."

Because they'd bolted from the studio as quickly

as possible, she was still wearing the navy jersey dress; since it wasn't as expensive as the gowns, they'd figured *Rate the Dates* wouldn't mind if it were returned to costuming tomorrow.

"You look happy," he remarked, nuzzling his face against her shoulder, the fabric of the dress feeling as soft as velvet. A hand still in her hair, he stroked the fine strands, feeling smooth between his fingers. She was silent now, but on the drive to the hotel, she'd chattered nonstop, full of ideas about reopening her business.

Yes, she looked happy…and so forgiving that everything inside Cash suddenly stilled. If there was ever a moment to explain why he'd really come to New York, this was it. He didn't want to keep secrets from this woman, not when she evoked such complex emotions, making him feel tangled up inside, ripped apart, tender and sweet and then eaten up with passion.

Surely, she'd respond with understanding. He parted his lips to speak…but to say what exactly? That a few weeks ago, he'd come to New York half thinking he might kill a man….

Her eyes were searching his. "What?"

He told himself he didn't want to ruin the romance, but he knew it was a lie. He was afraid of losing her by telling the truth. "I've been waiting all night to be here with you."

"Me, too."

Splaying his fingers, he thrust them up from her nape, thinking he'd make love to her first…soften her…make her predisposed to hear him out. But that was a lie, too. When she knew more, she'd walk away….

"I need you," Cash murmured, taking her mouth again. He needed to be inside her, to feel her legs tight around him, to feel her holding on to him as if she never meant to let go. Especially tonight. Because this would never last. The end hadn't yet played out, but the game was over. Soon enough, she'd find herself looking into smoke and mirrors.

His legitimate business was done. He should just get the hell out now. With her, he'd played a dangerous game, maybe the most dangerous of his life. How had the stakes risen to include his heart? Had he really thought he could use her, the way he'd used her twin?

Breaking the kiss, he dropped his gaze to breasts straining the fabric, hungry for his hands and mouth. How could he put his feelings into words? How could he tell her that the week had changed him? "When I saw you—" His voice caught, sounding rusty in the silence. "I wanted you."

"At the club?"

Nodding, he smoothed back her hair, registering that anger flowed out of him every time he looked at her. He was easygoing on the surface, but his deeper nature was volatile, so explosive he sometimes worried about what he might do. When he looked at Marley, though, calm came over him, as if he knew instinctively that she could tame the aggression with which he struggled.

Covering her mouth with his once more, he felt her arch, her response immediate, her hips locking with his, her lips parting for a more thorough kiss, her tongue parrying. Releasing a satisfied sound, he felt his mind go into the gray zone as her pelvic bone softened, molding to the ridge of his arousal. Groaning, he broke the kiss, leaned, grasped the hem of her dress and drew it over her head.

His breath caught as he dropped it. The dress had been lined, there was very little beneath, and heat ate up each inch of his skin, his groin aching with fierce pangs as his gaze fell on white bikini panties and a matching bra. Seeing the pink of taut nipples pushing through scanty lace, he groaned once more as he fell to her, tonguing her through fabric, biting gently at the nipples, catching them between his teeth and pulling, sending her head reeling back in ecstasy.

Yes…he'd learned how to touch her this week. She liked having the heavy swells of her breasts kneaded, the painfully erect tips pinched. She liked them touched almost roughly, to feel them raked with the prickly stubble of his chin. She liked having her belly rubbed with his palms, too, the hard heel of his hands moving lower, kneading her mound, the backs of his fingers caressing her thighs after she opened…until he was teasing between her legs, making her whimper as each wet stroke parted her, his glistening finger exploring her innermost secrets.

He liked it, too. Crouching between legs so toned, he loved how she let him bend them at the knees, her toes pointing and curling in desire as he lifted them higher, his eyes searing each inch of her. He loved entering her that way, feeling the relentless onslaught of climbing need as he watched his own burning flesh go inside ever so slowly, his heart stuttering as he buried himself in her breathtaking damp heat.

He was hard and wanting now. Leaning back, he unbuttoned and shrugged off his shirt. Memory mixed with their kiss, and as his hand found his fly and tugged down the zipper, he winced. He'd gotten so big for her that his jeans were painfully confining. Grunting softly, he registered relief as the zipper hit bottom and he bulged through the opening....

"Here," she panted. Her hands were on him now...helping and hurting him, each brush of her fingers sending shocks of longing through his system. As she pushed down his jeans, her mouth slammed to his again, and his hand suddenly groped, curling around her neck, urging back her head to better kiss her. He stepped from his jeans and briefs, and urged her from her panties, the sensation dark and desperate as her fingers surrounded his rigid flesh, his tongue turning wild against hers, his hand stroking between her legs where she was slick for him, burning.

Breaking the crazy-wet kiss, he shuddered, needing to watch her reaction as he pressed a finger inside her enveloping heat—her eyes faltering, nearly shutting, the lashes fluttering as if she were a dreamer trying to awaken. He pushed deeper inside, twisting his hand, exploring her inner flesh.

Reaching behind herself, she unhooked her bra from the back, and as the catch gave, her breasts swelled, spilled. Catching one with his mouth, his lips locked over a nipple as the straps slipped down her arms, his other hand exploring below, stoking a fire that ignited on her skin. Her mouth, no longer covered by his, unleashed cries on his shoulders before she kissed them, swirling her tongue on bare skin.

This was already more than he could take, but he pushed two fingers inside now, anyway. Groaning, he felt the greedy suckling of her flesh as she arched in rhythm, rising to meet the fingers as he thrust....

Backing toward the high bed, he pulled her with him, then seated himself and fumbled for protection. She was still standing, her skin pink and damp, dusky with desire, and when he bent to kiss her belly, his nostrils flared. Catching her female scent, his mind blanked, going dark; it was like a room in which the light had been extinguished.

Grasping her hips, he urged her onto his lap where she could straddle him. "I thought about this all night," he whispered as her legs circled his back.

Vaguely, he knew there were things he had to tell her, but right now, she was poised above him, and he was vanishing into her flesh. Damp palms squeezed his shoulders—she was using them to support herself—and her labored pants and catching breath sounded like music, a song he'd heard and forgotten, both familiar and yet new.

"More," he managed to whisper. "Take more, Marley. All of it. All of me." Sweat had turned his body slick. He pulled her down farther, his fingers tightening on her hips, dragging her deeper, bringing the edge closer.

Her hot, greedy mouth found his, and his hands molded her backside, guiding her. She was taking what she needed and he was loving it. They both wanted more, to ride harder, faster.... He arched to meet her, her whole body bouncing sexily as she climbed.

"C'mon," he whispered, his eyes roving over her as she rocked, her eyes half-shut, her cheeks flushed, the pink of her tongue darting to lick dry lips. "Do it for me," he whispered huskily, his drawl like thickened sugar. "Let me see you come."

She was so close. Her thighs slammed his—straining, taut, squeezing. She was naked, exposed, open. He bit his lower lip, holding back, crushing tenderness claiming him as he waited for her, feeling he wouldn't…he couldn't…

An animal cry ripped from his lips. "Come," he demanded hoarsely. He was a second away. But he wanted, needed, to feel her get off….

When pure burning fire convulsed around him in a glove of constricting heat, another cry was forced from his lips. Everything became madness then. Lips touching. Sounds of gasping, groaning…

Suddenly, his eyes slammed shut. "Marley," he gasped as she catapulted him over the top.

10

MARLEY STARTLED AWAKE, rapidly blinking her eyes before opening them fully, then she glanced around the room smiling, her first thought being that Granny Ginny had been wrong. *I'm blessed*, she thought triumphantly. Not *cursed*. No, definitely not. Of course Marley had gotten divorced. Cash was right—half of America divorced—but that hardly proved Marley would never find happiness in love. Where was Cash, though? The bed was wrecked from lovemaking—the duvet and pillows were on the floor—but she didn't hear the shower running.

"The phone," she whispered, pulling the sheet with her as she rose from bed, found her handbag and fumbled for the cell. Clicking it on, she said, "Marley Benning speaking."

"It's Edie. *Rate the Dates* found out it was you!"

"What?" she asked, realizing Cash's jeans weren't on the floor, which meant he'd probably worn them wherever he'd gone.

"The videographer assigned to you," Edie was saying. "Vinny Marcel. He realized you were pretending to be me. He was following you and Cash when you came to see Granny, and I guess he must have seen me standing around the building also, and put two and two together. I just got a call from Trevor Milane. He was trying to reach you at home, so I gave him your cell number. He said they're going to announce this on next Monday's show."

Marley groaned. "We were outed. I was afraid this would happen." Her heart missed a beat as she contemplated the news, then she frowned. Why had Cash left? He was supposed to take her to her apartment to change, then to the Dardens'.

"The audience voted on your dates, so Trevor said the prize money's not an issue."

"At least we can use it for our businesses, sis."

Edie sounded worried. "I think they're going to make me out to be the old cliché. You know, the wedding planner who never marries. And what if they discover we're all affected by a wedding curse? I mean, they found out I dated Cash before you did. They're doing a lot of sniffing around."

Edie continued. "And I've been getting so many new clients who called because they were watching the show. They want a planner associated with Julia Darden, but they also said they want me because I'm a romantic at heart."

It was the irony of ironies. "You are." Marley was the cynic.

"Well, no one would believe it now, and I can't afford to lose these clients, Marley. What am I going to do?"

"Maybe I can talk Trevor out of the announcement," Marley promised. Just as she disconnected, the cell rang again. She clicked on just as her eyes landed on a scribbled note on the table, probably from Cash. That was good. "Hello? Trevor?"

"How did you know?"

"Just a guess. I heard everything from Edie."

"I just called to say you won't lose the prize money."

"Thanks, but—" Marley plunged into a detailed explanation of how the mix-up had occurred, recalling the treatment she'd received on her arrival at the studio and reminding Trevor of how she'd tried to leave, then she finished by saying, "Really, if *Rate the Dates* had listened to me, this never would have happened, so you owe it to us. As it is, the American public doesn't know about the switch, and I don't see why they need to."

"Because it'll make ratings skyrocket," explained Trevor. "Especially when we talk about the wedding curse in your family."

Marley gasped. "You wouldn't! How did you find that out?"

"We have researchers working around the clock," he returned, "and that's really why I'm calling. I was hoping you'd verify some of the information our team uncovered regarding your...uh..." When he paused, she could hear papers rustling, then he said, "Ah. Here it is. Your Granny Ginny."

"No!" Marley groaned. Was all of America about to become privy to the Benning curse? "If you'd listened to me, alternates could have gone on the air. This is your fault."

"Look. We'll talk again," Trevor said, cutting her off.

Just as she was rudely disconnected, the cell rang yet again. No doubt it was Edie, calling to find out what Trevor had said. In a flash fantasy, Marley saw Cash coming through the door, looking like heaven and bearing lattes, but then, why would Cash go out for coffee when they could order room service?

Her stomach rumbled as she pressed Talk. "Hello? Edie?"

"Uh...no. Sam Beaujolais."

Who? "Oh," she suddenly said, remembering. Cash's ex-partner from the New Orleans precinct. It seemed so long ago—years—since she'd been told his name, even though it was really only days. Had she really not trusted Cash? Had she let Chris's betrayal nearly ruin such a promising relationship? She felt a delicious ripple of awareness go through her. Everything in her mind vanished, except the recollection of Cash's touch.

"Sam. I called you a few days ago," she prompted.

"From New York City?" he drawled.

His tone was better than caffeine. Something in it brought her more fully awake and propelled her steps toward the table and note. "Uh...yes." Was it Marley's imagination, or had his tone indicated something was wrong? "I live in New York. Well," she conceded, "not the city. Brooklyn."

"And you're a friend of Cash Champagne's?" He sounded dubious.

"Sort of. I mean, he was dating my sister, but..." Telling a stranger that sex just hadn't been happening between Edie and Cash didn't seem too kosher, so she changed tracks and said, "Uh...I'm in his hotel room right now. It's a long story, but we wound up on a show called *Rate the Dates*—"

"I heard. I've been on my fishing boat for a week, taking no calls, not even for emergencies, otherwise I would have known before now, and Annie—that's

Cash's manager, Annie Dean—she only now heard about the show…."

She waited through a long pause, then said, "So…?"

He hesitated. "You're connected to the Dardens?"

Her senses heightened. "My sister's planning her wedding, and I give Julia Darden workouts. Is there a problem? Cash has been…" Her eyes darted around the room. He really wasn't here. Why had he left?

"Uh…I hate to say this, and maybe I shouldn't," Sam Beaujolais continued kindly. "But you need to be careful. It's not my place to say anything, but Cash and Sparky Darden have a history. When Cash found out about Julia's wedding, he was threatening to go to New York and, well…"

"History?"

Her first thought was that Cash and Julia had been lovers, and that Sparky hadn't allowed Julia to pursue the relationship, but in that case, Sparky would have recognized Cash, right?

"When he found out about Julia Darden's wedding," Sam was saying, "I made Cash swear he wouldn't go to New York. You see, about fifteen years ago, Cash sneaked onto the man's Long Island property and…and, well, he almost killed him."

Marley stumbled toward the note on the table, thinking of the shots fired in the woods and Cash's fast response time. But she'd seen the shooter, right? Could her eyes have deceived her? He was far away, wearing a mask, she'd thought. Could it have been Cash? He'd been kneeling by tire tracks when she'd reached the highway, but she hadn't seen the SUV herself. "He tried to kill him? Why?"

"It's a long story," Sam said, "and not mine to tell,

but just to be on the safe side, we need to find Cash right now…."

No joke. What was it with these southerners? They all talked slower than snails moved. *Killed him?* The words were still registering as her eyes scanned a note that said, *Sorry, I'm afraid you'll never forgive me, but I've got to take care of some business at the Dardens'.*

"Is Cash there?" Sam was saying.

"Uh…no," she managed to say. Questions raced through her mind that no one was going to answer. Why had Julia's wedding sparked Cash's interest? What was his connection to the heiress? Dammit. Every warning signal she'd felt at the comedy club was justified. "He's not here!"

"Do you know where he is?"

She grabbed her dress from the floor, thinking she had to call Pete Shriver. How long had Cash been gone? Was he going to try to kill Sparky Darden again? Why? "He's at the Dardens'!"

"Hurry!" Marley begged the cab driver nearly an hour later, speaking through the closed Plexiglas partition, blinking back tears and pointing at the back of Cash's truck. "That's him! We're catching up!" The truck was far ahead, barely visible, slowing as it reached the estate's wrought-iron gates so Cash could talk to the occupant of the guard booth.

Marley fought the urge to throw her phone aside. It had been useless! Julia wasn't answering her cell, and the main residence was unlisted and Marley had left the number at home. Edie was no longer available, probably with a client. At last Marley had called 911. But she'd expected the road to be crawling with officers. Had they stopped Cash already? Had he sweet-talked them? Used identification he still carried to show he'd been a cop, just like them? She'd told the 911 operator that Cash had already made one attempt on Sparky Darden's life, so why was no one here?

Her blood pumped with fear. And anger. If Cash hadn't been using her to get close to Sparky Darden, then why hadn't he told her about his past history with Sparky? And if they had a past, why hadn't Sparky recognized him? She'd been wrong to rationalize her distrust as caused by her ex. No wonder Cash would just as soon date her as Edie! One sister was just as good as another—if a man's motive was to get close to a famous family...

And kill. Tears pushed at her eyes. This couldn't be possible! She'd made love to Cash. Kissed him, held him. He wouldn't harm anyone. It had to be a lie. But Cash's own partner said Sparky was in danger....

Marley's mind ran wild. Pete had said Julia's stalker might be a past associate of her father's. Had Cash worked for Sparky? Emotions overwhelmed her, but she couldn't afford to heed them. She'd never be able to live with herself if her own bad judgment caused someone harm. Especially Julia. She was so nice. Yes, Cash had snowed her. His using Marley to get onto Darden property—the only logical conclusion—and maybe to commit a murder, made her and Edie's problem with *Rate the Dates* look comical.

She'd been betrayed before, she told herself. She could handle this. But underneath, she was breaking. She'd done what she'd vowed she'd never do and trusted again, but Granny was right. There was a curse on the Bennings. Nothing else could explain this. How many times could a girl screw up when it came to love? She watched as Cash's truck stopped by the guard booth.

"Do you have a weapon in the car?" she yelled through the partition. Since cab-driving was the most dangerous occupation in New York, most drivers at least carried Mace.

The streetwise-looking man, whose identification photo announced a last name Marley associated with war-torn countries, had already recognized her from *Rate the Dates.* Now he said in broken English, "May you...if I ask why?"

That meant yes. Not that Marley didn't also have a repertoire of self-defense maneuvers. Quickly, she plunged into an explanation, assuring the man that he could help save a life. But whose? Was Julia the target? Or Sparky?

"They're letting Cash through the gate," she managed to say, feeling reduced to ineffectually narrating Cash's movements. Her throat was bone-dry. "Where are the cops?" she muttered again, pushing aside her hurt and perching on the edge of the ripped vinyl seat, one hand pressed against the partition for balance, the other still clutching her phone. She watched in horror as the truck continued, passing through the gate.

"What's going on?" she cried in panic. It was as if the Dardens' had been expecting him, but she'd called 911! She'd specifically told the officers to contact Pete Shriver, head of security. Now she was losing sight of the truck as it veered off the main driveway, striking terror into her heart, since the path he'd chosen led to a private entrance to Sparky's study.

"Oh, no," she whispered. She'd been having so many fantasies about a future with Cash. He lived in New Orleans, but he had business in New York, too. And secretly, she'd thought that if she used the *Rate the Dates* prize money to reopen her club, maybe she could open yet another in the South....

Her eyes were stinging, making her face burn. As the cab glided beside the guard booth, she rolled down the window and leaned out her head, hoping it was someone who'd recognize her, maybe Pete.

It wasn't. "I'm Marley," she croaked, her voice hoarse from stress. "Marley Benning. Julia's trainer. I called the cops. I thought they would be here. I think the man you just let through is going to kill Mr. Darden."

The woman in the booth merely stared at her as if she were crazy, and Marley's heart missed a beat. What was wrong with these people? Why couldn't anyone understand what she was saying? Why was no one helping? Hadn't she clearly stated that a man's life was in danger?

Everything was moving in slow motion. The woman said, "Can I see some ID? I'll have to call the house to announce you."

Marley gaped as she clawed through her handbag, then thrust out a fitness-club card left over from Fancy Abs.

"Do you have a license?"

"It's New York," she said. "I don't drive."

She watched in horror as the woman turned away, lifted a phone receiver, dialed and began to speak in hushed tones. Helplessly, she stared at the wrought-iron gates that had closed after Cash. They seemed miles tall. The cab could hardly crash through. Other than waiting, the only other option was to back down the drive, circle the property and find the same highway access Julia's stalker had used, but that would take longer.

Yes, Cash was definitely headed to Sparky's study, which could be reached from inside the house or from a flagstone patio. French doors opened onto a paneled room, decorated with old marble tables, settees and a fireplace. Was that where Sparky was going to die?

Gaping at the guard, her eyes bugging, Marley had never felt so completely powerless, not even when Chris had left. The guard was still talking, seemingly trying to get clearance, and Marley could only force herself not to imagine what was going on inside the house....

CASH STOOD IN THE DOORWAY a moment and watched as Sparky turned away from the fire he'd just stoked, placed the poker in a rack holding fire tools, then shoved his liver-spotted hands into the pockets of a crimson robe. After all these years, was he really going to confront the man who was his father?

"So," Sparky said slowly, his steely eyes watchfully assessing Cash, "did you come to kill me or not this time?"

One thing Cash would say for Sparky Darden, the man never lost his nerve. Maybe Cash looked as collected as the old man, but he didn't feel it. His heart was hammering against his rib cage. His knees felt weak. Sweat was starting to bead between his shoulder blades. He felt the way he did every time he looked at Marley Benning, if for completely different reasons.

"I'm still deciding," Cash finally returned.

"Would you care for a drink while you think it over?"

"At this hour of the morning?"

"No time like the present." When Cash didn't immediately respond, Sparky added, "If you don't kill me, I'm going to die, anyway. No doubt, you've figured that much out during the time you've been using the Benning girls to get close to me. Since I'm sick, anyway, I keep whiskey in my study even though the doctors forbid it."

Cash considered. "You talked me into it."

As Sparky headed for a roller cart and poured two shots into highball glasses, Cash crossed the room, stopping near the mantle where Sparky had been standing. An employee of the Dardens' had already taken Cash's coat, and now he could feel the fire's heat seeping through his clothes. The warmth made him think of Marley, who was still in bed at the Four Seasons, and even warmer than the fire.

"Here's to you," Sparky said, hobbling closer, drinks in both hands. He stopped in front of Cash, who took a glass, then both men turned toward the flames, preferring to look at them instead of each other. Usually, whenever Cash imagined meeting Sparky again, he had a knife in his hand. But after the week he'd spent with Marley, everything seemed so different....

And Sparky really was dying. Cash hadn't expected that. The man hadn't thrown him out, either. No, when he'd called earlier this morning from the

Four Seasons, briefly explaining why he wanted to visit, he'd imagined bloodshed. At least some shouting. Not two men sipping whiskey on a cold winter's morning, staring between tongues of fire and the snow-laden woods beyond a set of French doors.

Lifting his glass, Cash sipped again, feeling glad, somehow, for the burn of the liquid on his lips. "You're not going to ask me to leave? Or threaten to have me arrested?"

Sparky raised his eyes a second, then stared into the flames again, his gaze hard, his lips pursed, a tick visible in his cheek. "I'm sorry about doing that in the past," he apologized gruffly.

Under other circumstances, Cash might have smiled. Really, it was almost comical. Two rough-and-tumble type men trying to talk when they had little experience dealing with their emotions. But Cash didn't laugh. Instead, he knocked back another sip of whiskey.

"In a minute," Sparky suddenly said, as if deciding some female company might help them out, "I want to call Julia down here. But right now..." He cleared his throat. "Hell," he said abruptly. "I don't know what to say, Cash Champagne, and maybe there's no decent explanation. Years ago, women used to come at me with all kinds of paternity suits, you see, and so when you came around, saying you were my son..."

Cash's hackles started to rise, at least until Sparky continued. "I'd been used to turning people away, and no one, when investigated, had really turned out to be related. All of them just wanted money." Pausing, he sighed. "When you've got money, you learn a lot about the lies people will tell to get it."

"What about your lies?" Cash couldn't help but ask softly.

"Oh, I told plenty. Plenty more, to hold on to the money I'd made," the old man admitted. "And maybe that's why, at first, I didn't want to believe you. Besides, I'd lost my wife, and made a life with Julia…."

A life in which Cash had no place. What the hell had he been thinking? "I shouldn't have come here like that," Cash found himself murmuring. Over the past few days, when he'd visited the estate with Marley, he'd realized the old man regretted the mistakes of his past and was trying to rectify them. That had helped soften Cash's heart. "I was angry. My mother had just died. And she'd told me you were my…"

"Father?"

Cash nodded. "She'd been so sick, and our resources were so limited, and I kept thinking that if I'd known, if you'd given me some money…" But now he knew it was a lie. Cash's own mother had died of cancer, and while Sparky was alive, he was fighting the disease. Money wouldn't have helped.

As if reading his mind, Sparky softly said, "Death takes us all in the end, son. In that, we're all alike."

Cash took a deep breath, barely able to believe he was having this conversation—not with this man, not on the same ground where he'd once almost killed him.

"Shortly after you left that night," Sparky began again, "I felt bad about the way I sent you packing. It occurred to me that maybe you weren't lying. Maybe you really were my…blood. My son. But everything had happened so fast. In the heat of the moment, I hadn't wanted to know. And as soon as I said you could go, you ran."

"I realized you could prosecute me," Cash said. "Ruin my life. And I was mad. Really mad. I could only think of the life I could have led if…" If Sparky had recognized him as a legitimate child. Somehow, Cash couldn't bring himself to say the words. Thankfully, he didn't have to.

"I hired a private eye, but he never found you. Until now. Or at least he thought he had. He wasn't sure. He'd traced you to a place in New Orleans called the Cash Cow, and a month ago, he was headed down there to take some pictures of you, to see if you were really the same guy. It was dark, and your face was blackened, but we hoped to find similarities between you and the man on the security tape."

Cash's heart missed a beat. "Heavy guy," he said. "Short. About five-seven. Brown hair and a neatly trimmed mustache."

"That's him. Barry Kocot." Sparky raised an eyebrow appreciatively. "You're good. I'd heard you were a cop."

"He was drinking in my bar. I thought he was taking pictures of me, using a digital camera in his cell phone."

"He never got the pictures to me. His cell got ripped off before he could send them, and when he went back to take some more, you were gone."

He'd left to come here. "I'd seen the announcement about Julia's wedding," he admitted. "And it choked up the past. I got angry all over again, even though I hadn't felt that way for years, and I decided to come back." And then, deep down, where all his voiceless secrets lived inside him, he supposed he'd started to wonder about the man who'd come to snap pictures of him, too.

Sparky was eyeing him. "I didn't do the right thing, the first time you came," he said slowly. "But I looked for you. And Julia's been heartsick, knowing she's got a brother. She hated being an only child, you know. I didn't realize it was you until last night. Something about the way you moved on TV reminded me of the guy in the tape, and I told Julia what I suspected."

They'd looked for him. They wanted him. They were sorry for how their intertwined past had played out. Suddenly, Cash let the information flow over him. And he couldn't breathe. His chest felt tight. Floodgates opened and he wasn't exactly sure what he said next, except that it was about how he'd tried to use Edie to get a closer glimpse of Sparky, to find out about him, but then Edie and Marley had wound up switching places on the show. And then loving Marley had taken away his anger and pain....

When he was finished, Sparky said, "We want to get to know you, Cash. We want a relationship. You're my son. Julia's brother. Before I die, I'm doing everything I can to make all my amends, set things right...."

His voice trailed off, and then he said, "Do you mind if Julia joins us?"

Cash had imagined a thousand scenarios. This hadn't been one of them. But he shook his head and said, "Not at all. I think I'd...like to meet my sister." He paused. "On those terms."

HOURS SEEMED TO HAVE PASSED. More likely, it was ten minutes. But that was so long! Marley thought. What was going on? Everything about the guard seemed to move in slow motion—her lips, her hands as she returned the phone receiver to its cradle. The guard drew back the partition between her and the cab.

"Mr. Darden's in danger!" Marley urged. At least Marley hadn't heard a gunshot yet. Given the size of the Dardens' staff, somebody would have discovered Mr. Darden's body by now if Cash had really killed him, she told herself.

"You can go through now," the guard said.

Marley waited as the cumbersome electronic gates opened, and as the driver punched the gas, she said, "The access road winds around to Mr. Darden's study."

Heartbeats passed. Then she saw Cash's truck, abandoned on the road. The night had warmed, melting the snow, and footsteps led across the dusting, trailing soggy mud to a flagstone porch. The French doors were wide open! Why hadn't someone shut them? Were Cash and Sparky fighting inside? "Here!" she exclaimed.

As the cab came to a halt, she pushed open the door. Only when the strap of her handbag caught on the handle did she realize it was on her shoulder and that the phone was in her hand. As she tossed both items aside, a long arm came through the driver's window, then the man flicked his wrist, opening a knife. "Here," he said, the four-inch blade glistening.

"Thanks." Her grip closed around the handle, then Marley whirled, her eyes on the French doors.

Fury burst within her and she started to run. How could he have used her? He'd known about her history with Chris, but he'd betrayed her, anyway. Her legs pumped faster. Maybe their chemistry had nothing to do with why he'd chosen her over Edie to get close to the Dardens. Maybe he'd done so because she was such an obvious mark.

Well, she'd show him. Her feet were losing traction since she was unaccustomed to wearing dress flats, though. Why were the doors open? Why hadn't Pete Shriver locked them? She could see into the room now. Sparky crossed to the fire, hands thrust into the pockets of a long crimson robe. He was alive!

"Mr. Darden!" She tried to yell, but only a hoarse rasp sounded. Now she saw Cash. He was coming up behind Sparky, carrying a sharp blackened poker! He began to raise it.... Her feet left the grass, skidded across flagstones, then hit a carpet. Clutching the knife harder, she sprawled, then regained her footing, lunging toward Sparky, crying, "Get away from him, Mr. Darden! Don't kill him, Cash!"

Cash turned slowly. "Kill him?"

Hunkered over, gasping and waving the knife, her heart hammering, Marley suddenly realized others were in the room. Pete was near the door. Julia was seated on Lorenzo's lap on a sofa next to a marble table laid with a silver service. She was sniffling, pressing tissues to her eyes as tears streamed down her face. Behind Marley, her footprints tracked across a carpet that had been whiter than Caribbean sand. She watched in stupefaction as Cash lowered the poker, stoked the fire, then returned the poker to a rack.

Sparky clamped his hand on Cash's shoulder.

"Sorry to give you such a start," Sparky said. "Before he even got here, the cops came by, saying you'd called nine-one-one, and when we tried to call your cell phone, it was busy. There's no danger here, young lady."

"There's not?"

Sparky shook his head. "I didn't figure Cash would try to kill me. But if he did, Pete was here." He paused. "This may come as a surprise, but Cash is my son, and…" He stared at her a minute. "Now, are you Marley or Edie?"

"Marley."

Sparky nodded. "So, you're the one who's dating Cash? You were pretending to be your sister on the show?"

She wasn't about to go into that right now. "Your *son?*"

"Isn't it the sweetest thing you've ever heard?" cried Julia. "He's my brother! When he called this morning, to explain everything, and to say he'd been coming out here, to get to know us—" Julia bit back a sob "—and that he forgave Daddy, and wanted to drop by this morning and talk to us even more…." Pausing, Julia pressed the tissue to her eyes. "Well, it was awkward. And I guess when he got here, he was still mad enough to kill Daddy. But he said a woman had changed him— which must mean you—and now he isn't nearly as mad as he was before. You know," Julia clarified, "years ago, he tried to kill Daddy. And to think that Daddy and I never believed we'd find him…."

Marley could only stare. "What?"

"Oh, I've been rumored to have plenty of illegitimate kids over the years," Sparky said, "and when I was younger, I never asked too many questions about the claims, since most of the women were just lying to get my money. Because of that, when DNA testing began, most of the paternity claims stopped, naturally. But this boy...well, he's really my flesh and blood." Sparky drew a deep breath.

"Sure," he continued, "when Julia first started getting the threats, I suspected he might have something to do with them, but he doesn't. The perp could be so many people I've hurt over the years. Ever since I got the big C, I've been trying to right my wrongs, including tracking down this son of mine. That's how we hooked up, by the way."

"We?" Marley managed to say. "As in you and me?"

Sparky nodded. "Years ago, your daddy used to work with me in the catering business. That Joe Benning," he recalled with a sudden grin and wistful sigh. "When I got my big break, and bought my first hotel, a run-down fleabag in the Bowery, I knew I ought to take Joe with me to the top."

Marley couldn't believe any of this. "You worked with Pop?"

"More than worked. We were pals. I was older, but we liked to chew the fat. I was afraid to share my big break, though. Your old man was too smart, and I was afraid of the competition. I can admit that now. I could have helped that young man make a whole other life."

Still in shock, Marley was starting to get a little offended. "My pop's done pretty well for himself."

Sparky shrugged, turning to Pete. "Can you shut those doors. It's getting cold." As Pete responded, Sparky explained. "When I built the fire, it got smoky. Overly warm, too, but now it seems fine."

So, Cash hadn't used the doors to gain illegal access? No more than he'd meant to kill Sparky with the poker? Marley's mind was still reeling, so she listened as Sparky returned to his monologue. "Your father's done well, all right, especially if his daughters are an indication." Suddenly, he laughed. "Yes, sir. You sure started a scene, Marley. The cops came here, must have been ten cars with their sirens wailing, thinking Cash was trying to kill me, and just as soon as they left, Cash showed up. And then you came in with a knife to save my life!"

"But a man named Sam Beaujolais said Cash tried to kill you in the past," she muttered, steadfastly avoiding Cash's gaze, unwilling to look at him until she got a full explanation.

"About fifteen years ago," Sparky assured. "He turned up on the veranda, dressed in dark clothes, his face blackened, so I could barely see him. He tripped the alarms, knocked on the front door, and when I opened it, he came at me with a knife just like the one in your hand.

"The security staff subdued him, but he'd only talk to me, and when he told me why he was mad enough to kill, I let him go.

"And I've regretted that ever since. After I started fighting cancer, I wanted to talk to him, but I didn't know his name, and so I sent private eyes to find him, but they never did...." Sparky sighed. "My own attitude was the problem, of course, how I would never help people, never get involved. When I got sick, I had plenty of time to think. I'd stay up all night watching those late-night infomercials...."

"Which is how you saw my sister?" Marley

guessed, her jaw slackening. So, her father must have known there was a connection between him and Sparky Darden, and that Edie's landing the Darden wedding wasn't just happenstance. He hadn't said anything, not wanting to take away Edie's feelings of success. Marley's heart swelled. Her pop was one of a kind.

"When I saw Edie's infomercial," Sparky continued, "advertising her wedding planning business, I could see she had your old man's spunk, just like you do. I wanted to give Edie a chance, and when you came on board, I was glad it worked out for everybody."

Not really. Marley's lungs were still burning, and she didn't understand what was going on, not really. "But I just talked to Cash's ex-partner," she managed to say again. Her eyes shifted to Cash, and suddenly, she couldn't speak at all. No matter how hard she tried, she couldn't make a story out of this, not with a beginning, middle and end. Cash had tried to kill Sparky years ago, even though Sparky was his father, which made Julia Darden Cash's sister....

"Pete. Why don't you go out and pay that cab driver," said Sparky. "His engine's running. C'mon, Julia and Lorenzo. You two better help me to bed. CNN's on."

"CNN is always on, Daddy," Julia protested, not wanting to leave her brother, and to see whatever was about to happen between Marley and Cash.

Marley barely heard. She got the drift. Sparky was playing matchmaker, leaving her alone with Cash. Cash's eyes were so liquid, she realized now. Glistening. As if he was about to cry, but of course, he wouldn't because he was...a man's man. And an ex-cop. A club owner. And, well...Cash Champagne. Still, his dark eyes had sheen to them, not to mention a wounded look as if to say she—not he—was the issue here.

When everybody had left the room, he drawled, "Damn, Marley. Did you really call Sam Beaujolais?"

"Your club, too. I...felt something wasn't on the up-and-up." Her eyes hardened. "And I was right."

He frowned. "Were you really going to kill me?"

Realizing the knife was still in her hand, she glanced over her shoulder, through the French doors, but the cab was gliding away, and Pete was walking back toward the house, heading for another doorway. Realizing the Dardens had probably tipped well enough that the driver could buy himself a new weapon, she turned toward Cash again, only to discover he'd crossed the room so silently that she hadn't heard.

Gently, with his hand covering hers, he uncurled her fingers around the knife, then set it aside, the touch of his skin electric. Soft, too. Dry with warmth from the fire. And suddenly, she registered, more tender than she could bear. Unwanted tears were pushing at her lids again, welling beneath them. She inhaled sharply. "I thought..."

"I know what you thought, Marley." Turning her hand, he laid it palm to palm with his, then twined his fingers through hers and led her away from the drafty doors, toward the warmth of the fire. When they reached it, he let go of her, rested a hand on the mantle, and surveyed her. "You weren't far from wrong," he conceded.

Feeling shaky inside, not knowing what to believe, she crossed her arms and waited, wishing she didn't feel so betrayed. "I wasn't?"

Shaking his head, he looked away, into the fire, and she, too, watched the burning embers, hearing kindling snap in the silence, making tiny dots of burning red spiral upward. "My mother was a maid," he began. "In one of Sparky's hotels."

He'd told her that his mother was a maid, and that she'd died years ago, and even that she'd been a Johnny Cash fan, which was why she'd named him Cash. "She worked for Sparky?"

Flame-touched hair fell into his eyes as he continued to study the fire. "That's how I got my start in the restaurant-management business. When I was a kid, I'd follow her around, so I guess I got used to that kind of work. I always felt it was in my blood."

"And how," she couldn't help but say, thinking of Sparky.

He shrugged, and when he glanced at her, pain flared in his eyes like the fire, then died down like the embers. "But as far as I knew, I never had a father."

"No?" she urged, her heart leaping expectantly.

He blew out a long sigh. "Well...my mama told me he'd died in Vietnam." Shaking his head, this time ruefully, he added, "She never liked to talk about him, so I didn't ask many questions, but I read about the war and, at least in my mind, more than she ever knew, I came to have a picture of him, a sense of who he'd been."

She saw what was coming. "But he wasn't..."

"Real? No. She gave me the name Champagne, as if it was his, but she said she did so because having me made her feel as happy as when she sipped champagne." Cash eyed her, gauging her reaction, knowing she wanted to ask how he'd found out the truth. "About twenty years ago," he continued, "my mama was diagnosed with breast cancer that wasn't caught in time." He took another deep breath, his chest visibly expanding as he filled his lungs.

"Cancer? Just like Sparky?"

"Exactly," he drawled. "I cared for her a few years. It was slow and painful, and at the time...well, it was rough. I didn't have the money I've made since. I was barely twenty when she died. And so, I just did my best. Friends helped me. Sam Beaujolais practically moved in. So did Annie Dean, who manages my bar in New Orleans now.

"Right before she passed, my mama told me the truth." His eyes found hers again. "And I hit the roof. I'd known of Sparky Darden. He owned practically every hotel in the South, and I'd even taken paychecks from his establishments. When she broke down, and said she'd lied, and told me he was my real father..."

Marley could imagine. They'd been strapped for cash, and he'd been too young to feel competent as he tried to help a terminally ill parent. And then he'd found out his biological father—a man whose phantom he'd idealized—hadn't existed at all. He was really a wealthy, powerful man who'd abandoned them, who might have stepped in and done something to help.

"As soon as she passed, I took a flight here. I'd never been outside the French Quarter, much less New Orleans. Hell," he shrugged ruefully, "I'd never been on a plane or in a taxi...."

"You came here and tried to kill Sparky Darden?"

When he nodded confirmation, she didn't know whether to laugh or cry. Cry, she guessed because tears were plaguing her eyes again. Her heart went out to the young man trying to do his best in a situation that could have no good outcome, who'd idolized a war-vet father who'd never even existed, and who, as he'd lost one parent, also lost another…one he'd never really known he'd had. And then, to have the man you most hated show you mercy and not prosecute, and to be sent away from his real father's house….

"I'll understand if you don't forgive me," he murmured.

What was he talking about? Marley's eyes leaped to his. Her voice stalled, her throat constricting, but she guessed, "For using me to get onto the estate?"

Lifting his hand from the mantle, he reached for her, but his fingers only brushed her waist, as if he didn't dare pull her closer, his eyes filling with yearning. "I didn't use you, Marley. Edie, yes. I admit it. But not you…."

A tear tumbled over the rim of her eye. She took a step toward him, thinking they'd both been betrayed. What he'd undergone was so much worse than the bad decision she'd made to start a life with Chris. How could she have been so hard on this man? Now, she wanted to fold him in her arms, to make sure he got all the love he needed, the love the Dardens were so willing to give him now, too.

"I know you didn't," she murmured.

"When I saw you, it was different," he explained

as she stepped into his arms. "Not like with Edie. And when we kissed…"

"I know," she said simply. There was so much to tell him about what had happened with Edie and the show, but she'd worry about that later. Edie had always been her other half, but Cash might become her better half. "We've both suffered betrayal," she whispered. "We both have fathers we never knew."

"In the past," he murmured huskily. "That's why I left you sleeping and came out here. I called Sparky this morning, then came to face the old demons and see how things went."

"That's why you got onto the property so easily," she murmured.

His lips hovered close, right over hers. "Yeah… Pete may have asked them to stall you, so Sparky and I could talk. Sorry about that. When I got to New York this time, I really didn't know what I was going to do. Somebody had left a *Celebrity Weddings* magazine in my bar, and when I saw Julia's picture…"

"The picture of his legitimate child," Marley supplied.

"It choked up old feelings. Maybe I would have tried to kill him. I don't know." Pulling her closer, he brushed his mouth against hers, the touch hotter than fire. "Years ago, I forgave my mama for her lies. I know how much she loved me. She just wanted me to have a father." He sighed. "Lately, I realized a P.I. might be sniffing around my bar, looking for me. I used to be a cop, so he wasn't hard to spot. Deep down, even though I didn't admit it to myself, I was hoping Sparky had sent him."

"And it turned out to be true."

He nodded. "But I didn't know that then. And on the plane, I started wondering if there might be a way to get close to him, and find out what he was really like and if he'd changed."

"Before you tried to tell him who you were again?"

"Or kill him. I don't like to think of all the years my mama struggled, but then…" A smile curled his lips. "We didn't do badly, either. There was a lot of love in our house, just like in yours.

"When I came out here with you, I realized Sparky's changed. He was a weak man who needed to climb toward a goal that would never bring him the thing he most wanted."

She raised her eyebrows. "What?"

"Love." Cash paused, his voice turning husky. "What I feel for you, Marley. You took the anger out of me. I guess I just…fell for you."

Her throat closed. "You did?"

Nodding, he claimed her lips with sparks worthy of the fire, saying, "You changed my life."

She was aware of the wall she'd built around her heart when Chris had left. "Yesterday," she murmured, "something so ridiculous as Granny's story made me doubt my capacity for love."

Cash's betrayal had been so much greater than hers, though, his grief so much harder to bear, and yet he'd arrived intact, loving her. "You just changed my life, too," she murmured, and with the words, her heart swelled, breaking through the rest of that wall inside her. Just a week ago, she'd never have thought it could happen, but…

Leaning back enough to look into his eyes and communicate passion, she said, "I love you, too, Cash."

Right before his lips nestled to hers, Cash chuckled softly, saying, "No wedding curse, huh?"

Marley's response was very firm as she pressed closer, letting their hips lock, her arms tightening around his waist until heat surged between them. Staring into his eyes, she thought, *I'm definitely getting back in bed with this man. And maybe, just maybe, I'll even marry him.* "A curse?" she returned, feathering her lips across his, her eyes shutting with the promise of the moment. "Absolutely not, Cash Champagne."

* * * * *

Look for more BIG APPLE BRIDES *adventures!*

When her girlfriends oust her from a ski-share where she'd hoped to find her dream man, Bridget Benning has to admit Granny Ginny could be right about the Bennings being cursed....

Face it, Edie's been exposed nationally as the wedding planner who never dates, and Marley's in love with Cash, but who knows how long that will last? And how could jewelry designer Bridget have replicated an exact design of the engagement ring worn by the ghost bride of Hartley House, without ever having seen the ring?

Determined to ensure her own future prospects, Bridget has no choice but to play ghost-buster in Granny Ginny's haunted plantation house, even if it means taking an escort from the Big Apple to swamp country. So what if she and her longtime best friend, Dermott, are fish out of water? Of course, Bridget doesn't know that Dermott has his own ghost from the past to put to rest—Bridget herself! Tired of haunting her life and carrying his secret torch, Dermott is ready to move on....

But will the ghosts of Hartley House let him?

* * * * *

Look for NIGHTS IN WHITE SATIN,
Book 2 of the BIG APPLE BRIDES *miniseries*
by popular Jule McBride,
on sale in February 2005.

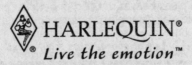

**Coming in February 2005
from**

Silhouette

Desire

Margaret Allison's
A SINGLE DEMAND
(Silhouette Desire #1637)

Cassie Edwards had gone to a tropical resort
to find corporate raider Steve Axon, but ended up
losing her virginity to a sexy bartender instead.
Cassie then returned home to a surprise:
her bartender *was* Steve Axon! Mixing business
with pleasure was not part of her plan, and
Cassie was determined to forget that night—
but Steve had another demand....

Available at your favorite retail outlet.